TREACHERY

Bernie Ziegner

The hit on Carmine occurred at the Scottsdale Saguaro Inn where he had a scheduled encounter with Laura Jenkins, a high-priced call girl. Laura, on her way to keep her prearranged appointment with Carmine, witnessed two hit men leaving his room. Although, she was not killed as a witness due to the sudden appearance of hotel guests, two days later a single gunman executed her as she tried to exit her car when she arrived home.

She had told of her experience at the hotel first to her friend Gina Rossi and then to Bob Wagner. Bob had tried to persuade Laura to stay with him to allow the situation to calm down. However, she had insisted on going home the next day. Bob did not know Laura intimately but had come to care about her and learning of her murder upset him greatly. A quest to avenge her death grew with time.

TREACHERY

Bernie Ziegner

© Bernie Ziegner.

All rights reserved. This book or any portion thereof may not be reproduced or used in any manner whatsoever without the express written permission of the publisher except for the use of brief quotations in a book review.

ISBN: 978-1-66785-569-1 (paperback)

ISBN: 978-1-66785-570-7 (eBook)

Other Novels by Bernie Ziegner

Timberline

Pursuit

Death in Cedar Canyon

Missing

Tapping in to Murder

Dark Horizon

Bushwhacked

Cienga Crossing

Murder at Tri-City Mall

Anomaly

CHAPTERS

Chapter 1	Explosion	1
Chapter 2	Explosion Investigated	3
Chapter 3	Laura in Trouble	7
Chapter 4	Christy Returned With Questions	10
Chapter 5	Laura at Bob's Office	14
Chapter 6	Laura Stays at Bob's Office	21
Chapter 7	Tragedy	25
Chapter 8	Christy Stops By	29
Chapter 9	Fraud Suspect	32
Chapter 10	Palumbo Suspects	38
Chapter 11	Ricardo's Pizza	41
Chapter 12	Reporter's Demise	46
Chapter 13	Nice Evening	51
Chapter 14	New Developments	53
Chapter 15	Sleuthing	56
Chapter 16	Bob's Recovery	64
Chapter 17	Understandings	69
Chapter 18	Next Steps	76
Chapter 19	BOLO	92

Chapter 20	Inquiries	98
Chapter 21	Paul Salerno	107
Chapter 22	Nick Carlucci and Michael Agouti	111
Chapter 23	What Now?	118
Chapter 24	Evidence	130
Chapter 25	The Meeting	137
Chapter 26	Indictments and Trial	141
Chapter 27	Post Indictments	145
Chapter 28	Post Trial	147
Chapter 29	Fire Insurance Claim	150
Chapter 30	Greg Held Captive	153
Chapter 31	Greg Rescued	160
Chapter 32	Rinaldi Fights Back	166
Chapter 33	Settlement	173
Chapter 34	Finale	178

CHAPTER 1

EXPLOSION

What the hell was that? Startled, he sat up in bed. The room was dark. A dream? Then he heard it again; an explosive boom shook his bed. He heard something hit the sliding-glass door to the small porch of his second floor apartment. Bob Wagner, heart racing, swung his legs out of bed. His feet groped for his well-worn slippers as he took a quick look at the glowing alarm clock and swore. It was 11:20 Friday night and he'd only been asleep an hour. The dinner with his new date had been nice; but there hadn't been any afterglow. Oh well.

He fumbled for the switch to the nightstand lamp. At the sliding-glass door, still only in his boxers, he pushed the drapes aside and slid the door open. The night air hadn't cooled much from the heat of the day. Outside, he felt the crunch of something hard underfoot and glanced down to see pieces of what looked like glass and metal. Black smoke and flame rose from a 'visitor parking' spot. He recalled a car parked there from time to time in the evenings, a white BMW. A well-dressed middle age man came with the car and he would disappear at the north entrance to the apartments. A little after dinner coziness, he wondered?

Better see what's going on. As he turned to go back inside, he saw flashing blue lights as two Scottsdale police cruisers raced into the parking lot. He could hear sirens approaching on the main street.

Bob tried not to step on debris of what he assumed were bits of wreckage from the explosion. Back inside, he hurriedly pulled on an ASU t-shirt and blue jeans and then slipped bare feet into loafers. He rushed down the stairs to the exit at the south end of the building, nearest to the explosion site. When he pushed open the glass door, a foul odor wafted toward him.

Acrid smoke kept the increasing number of onlookers from the apartments at a distance. The cacophony of sirens from arriving fire trucks and emergency vehicles with dozens of blue and red flashing lights lent an unreal aura to the parking lot. Curiosity aroused, he went closer to the wreck. Had there been someone in the car? How had the bomb been triggered? Was there someone in the crowd that had set off the bomb from a cell phone? A sudden flare up from under the rear of the wreck and Bob froze in his tracks. He started to back away. Flames and smoke now obscured any sight of the wreck. He heard a policeman shout a warning to him to get back to the building. He started coughing and backed away quickly.

CHAPTER 2
EXPLOSION INVESTIGATED

Christy Holland, detective sergeant, Scottsdale PD, arrived at the scene of the explosion in an unmarked car, dressed in civilian clothes with badge and gun at her waist. The call-out from her lieutenant to investigate a reported shooting at the rundown Cactus Flower Motel had turned out to be an old drunk celebrating the 4th of July several weeks early. A uniformed officer had seized the gun and facilitated a trip to the lock-up for the inebriated celebrant. On the way home she heard the calls for fire and explosion assistance. She turned on the blue and red lights at her windshield.

Christy parked well away from the emergency vehicles and the still arriving police cruisers. This was their show, she knew, but was also sure a crime had been committed. Christy took in a quick overview and acknowledged the officers on hand with a smile and comment. Then she started toward the apartment building, walking behind the gathering crowd with an eye to anyone acting suspicious.

She watched as a man was being directed by a police officer to move farther away from the explosion site. Two officers were setting up a yellow tape boundary. One officer again shouted for the man to move back and get out of the area being taped. The man, coughing, withdrew closer to the apartment building. People were still coming out of the building and crowded at the yellow tape.

Treachery | 3

Detective Holland looked at the man that had been directed to move back. Nothing about him aroused suspicion. He looked like he had a bad hair day or just got out of bed. But she acknowledged he was damn cute. "Sir, you are to stay behind the yellow tape."

He turned toward her as she approached and smiled. "Okay. Sorry."

She returned his smile. "I'm Detective Holland. You are?"

"Bob Wagner." He motioned with his thumb. "I live on the second floor. Explosion woke me up."

"What did you see from your apartment?"

"Well, I was asleep and something loud woke me up. About that time there was another explosion and I heard something hit my sliding glass door. I went out there, tried not to step on anything, and saw fire and smoke from what had been a car. As the police arrived, I put on some clothes and hurried down here to see what was happening."

"Did you see anyone near or walking away from the car?"

"No. People were starting to come out of the building."

Christy made a few notes in a small notebook. She looked at Bob. "Do I have your permission to inspect your balcony and glass door? I'd like to see what might have come from the explosion. Also, I might want to tell the fire inspector and bomb guys to take a look at your balcony." She knew the fire inspector would be doing a thorough job, but felt another set of eyes couldn't hurt, as this was a crime scene. Besides, he was definitely cute.

"Oh, sure."

- - - -

The attractive detective of maybe thirty years of age stirred a keen interest in Bob. Her off-blonde hair was up in a bun, but he imagined it would fall well below her shoulder if set free. Her voice, all business at the moment, had a seductive lilt. Her gaze from gray-green eyes toward him had been neutral, not challenging. He hoped his look at her hadn't been offensive.

Christy motioned for Bob to walk ahead of her up the stairs. He held open the fire door. She smiled and asked him to lead the way. They stopped in front of apartment 23 and Bob unlocked the door. She followed him inside and the door swung closed behind her. Bob stepped into the bedroom and then over to the sliding glass door to the balcony.

"Mr. Wagner, please stand to one side and let me take a look out there."

Bob stepped away. "Please, just Bob."

She nodded and grinned.

He watched Christy pull the sliding door open and step carefully onto the landing. Her black slacks fit snugly. Bob reluctantly shifted his gaze and left the bedroom. In the kitchen, he started the coffee maker.

- - - -

Christy looked at the objects that had landed on the balcony. Hopefully they'd be parts of the bomb and would give the bomb guys something to go on. The state bomb experts should arrive from Phoenix at any moment. Using her cell phone she took photos of the balcony door and flooring. She would leave the physical evidence for the fire inspector and bomb experts.

Back inside, Christy closed the sliding door, a quick glance around the room, and walked into the kitchen. "Bob, tell me again what you heard and experienced earlier."

"Sure." He glanced at her and then looked at the coffee maker. "I was awakened by something. It seemed like a loud boom. Then came another explosion and I heard stuff hitting the sliding glass door. I took a quick look outside, but I tried not to step on anything."

"Did you touch anything out there?"

He shook his head. "No."

"What did you see from the balcony? Did you see anyone?"

"Didn't see anyone until I was out of the building. Black smoke and flames came from what was left of the car." Bob reached for a cup and turned to Christy. "Would you like a cup of coffee? I need one to wake up."

Christy smiled. "Thanks, but no. I'm going to be quite busy. By the way, had you seen the car earlier that day?"

"I've seen a white BMW parked in that 'visitors' spot often. It was always in the evening."

"Have you seen the driver?"

"It's a middle-aged white man. He's always well dressed. I don't know the guy, but I've seen a man that looks like him at the far end of my hallway, down the hall from here at the north end of the building."

Christy made a few notes, smiled and thanked him for his cooperation. She pulled a card from her side pocket and handed it to him. "If you think of anything…"

"Okay, sure."

"Thanks again."

"You're welcome." He watched her walk to the door and leave. Hell of a good-looking woman.

CHAPTER 3
LAURA IN TROUBLE

Saturday afternoon Laura Jenkins went to meet her client, Carmine Palumbo, at a third floor room of the Scottsdale Saguaro Inn per their previous arrangement. She had been introduced two years ago to the aging but still powerful head of the Palumbo outfit at a Silk Parlor celebration. Carmine soon became her private client who easily afforded her top fee. She wore what he liked, black slacks and a well-fitted white silk blouse. He didn't care for a lot of bling, so she wore only simple gold earrings. Her long amber hair was up in a bun, at least until he loosened it.

When she exited the elevator she turned left and after a few steps, turned left again into the hall that led to room 309. As she walked down the hall, Laura saw two white men suddenly leave her client's room, still fifty feet in front of her. She heard the door slam closed behind them. One was over six feet tall with elbow patches on his brownish sport coat and he carried a briefcase. The other man was stocky at about five feet three inches wearing a team jacket, featuring a large letter 'B' in yellow and black on the back. The shorter man turned to look back and then said something. Both men stopped and turned toward her.

The two men seemed to have identical faces and she quickly realized they wore masks. Fearful now, she slowed her pace. A chill ran up her back as the two men stared at her. She stopped. Had something terrible happened to Carmine? She was saved from further interaction with them by the arrival of several noisy hotel guests down the hall behind her. The two men moved quickly to disappear into the nearby exit stairwell.

Laura couldn't gain entrance to her client's room by knocking on the door. When she used her cell phone to call into the room, there was no reply. With a sense of panic, she looked around for the two men and not seeing them quickly retraced her steps to the elevator. At the ground floor, she was relieved to not see anyone in the hallway.

Laura stopped to report the problem to the bar tender.

"Larry, I wasn't able to get Mr. Palumbo to open the door or answer his phone."

He stopped wiping the bar. "I wonder if he's ill or something."

"Maybe you could check on him?"

"Yeah, sure." He smiled. "You have time for a drink?"

"I've got to run." She hurried toward the exit.

She was afraid of the two men and of being involved in whatever happened to Carmine. Laura quickly departed the hotel and hurried to her car. Inside, she locked the doors and turned on the engine and the air conditioner. Her heart pounded. Sweat wet her brow. She didn't see anymore of the two men, and somewhat relieved drove straight home. Arriving at her apartment, she gave her friend and benefactor, Gina Rossi, a call.

"Gina, it's me, Laura."

"What's wrong? You didn't see your date?"

Laura related what she had experienced at the hotel and of her fear.

"You have to stay home tonight, forget the high rollers for a few days."

"Gina, I can't. I need to keep making money. You know that."

"Listen, stay home tonight and be at the Silk Parlor first thing in the morning. Will you do that?"

Laura's fear was heightened by the tone of Gina's voice and she promised to stay home.

Gina Rossi, an attractive woman of thirty five years, owned the Silk Parlor, a high-end social club located just north of downtown Scottsdale.

Gina and her staff organized parties at client companies as well as at the Silk Parlor by employing her models as hostesses. Parties were held on the premises to introduce influential and wealthy men and women to each other and to her hostesses. The ladies were recruited from night clubs, dance studios and gentlemen's clubs and were offered safe working conditions even if they made a bit less money. Gina insisted that there be no hanky-panky, as she called it, in the club. All personal interludes were to be away from the Silk Parlor.

Excellent food and beverage was prepared by a highly regarded catering service and presented at the parties for the enjoyment of the guests. Only the staff hostesses and invited guests are present during a social gathering at the Silk Parlor, thus offering a comfortable and easygoing atmosphere.

CHAPTER 4
CHRISTY RETURNED WITH QUESTIONS

Bob opened his apartment door late Saturday afternoon to firm knocking.

Christy smiled, "Hi. Would you mind answering a few more questions about the explosion?"

"Sure, it's nice to see you again," said Bob as he moved aside to let her enter. "Come in. I really don't remember anything new, though." He closed the door quickly trying to keep the hot afternoon air outside.

He marveled at how attractive she looked in plain but well fitting gray slacks with a white silk blouse and blue blazer. Her police shield and service pistol were clipped on her belt at her right hip. The blouse hugged her, not leaving much to the imagination as she moved. Her off-blonde hair was in a bun, and he wondered again how she would look with her hair down. His heart beat faster.

Both stood by the island in the kitchen. Christy cleared her throat. "Bob, you said you didn't know the man the car belonged to. I was wondering if a name had occurred to you, yet."

He shook his head. "I've seen the guy on this floor at the other end of the hallway, maybe visiting the last apartment."

"Does the name Jack Harvey mean anything to you?"

He shook his head. "Doesn't ring a bell."

"A woman by the name of Liz Thurston lives in the end apartment on this floor. Do you know her?"

"I've seen a blonde woman a few times at the far end of the hallway near the stairs. I didn't pay much attention. I don't know her."

"Liz Thurston is the name on the mailbox for the end apartment; and according to the manager, the woman lived there alone for the past eight months. However, no one answered the door when I knocked. The car she registered with the management, a red Mazda Miata, was not in the parking lot."

"I do recall a red Miata parked at the far end of the building. A blonde woman drove it."

"You never talked to her? You don't know anyone she was associated with?"

"No. I've seen her car at various times during the day and at night, coming and going. I don't know what kind of job she has."

Christy grinned. "Liz Thurston is employed at the FBI office in Phoenix."

"No kidding? What about the guy in the bombed out car?"

"Forensics got enough to identify him."

"It's the Jack Harvey guy you mentioned?"

She nodded. "We don't know a lot about him, yet. Except, as you say, he was probably friendly with Liz Thurston."

"Wonder if it was an irate spouse situation."

"Doubt it. She was divorced."

Christy's cell phone buzzed and she pulled it from her pocket. "Excuse me a second."

As she turned away to converse on her phone, Bob filled two cups with coffee and set a small creamer cup to the side. He didn't look at her, hoping she wouldn't stop him. He slid a cup to within her reach.

Treachery | 11

She closed the phone and stuffed it back into her pocket. "Well, I know a little more about Jack Harvey." She picked up the creamer and let a few drops into her coffee and took a sip. "Our boy was divorced and was a financial guy employed by Carmine Palumbo."

"Wow. A Palumbo guy with an FBI agent? I can't imagine that went over well with either Carmine or Frank."

"Uh-huh. That's probably why he isn't around anymore."

"That sure seems like a risky situation to get oneself into," said Bob as he brought his cup up to his lips. "Mr. Harvey, I mean."

"Near as anyone can tell, it's been going on for four months."

"He couldn't have been too bright to think someone in the Palumbo outfit wouldn't notice and pass it on to Carmine or Frank."

"You know those two gentlemen?"

Bob shook his head. "Did some insurance investigation for Frank — a car accident."

Christy took a sip of coffee and placed the cup back on the counter. "So, what kind of investigative work do you do? You work for an insurance agency?"

"No. I have a small office here in Scottsdale, Confidential Investigations. I go after fraudsters mainly."

"You don't do divorce work? Seems like that might be more profitable."

"I've had a few clients like that. I find it leaves a bad taste in my mouth. Mostly, I've been working with state agencies and insurance companies to investigate people they say are cheating on their claims."

"Does it pay?"

"Not a lot. Once in a while I'll hit a big one that gives a large bonus."

"Can you pull in other kind of work?"

Bob nodded slowly. "Maybe. I haven't looked into other opportunities too much. I stay rather busy these days. Why? You offering me a job?"

Christy chuckled. "Not today. But you never know."

Bob noticed Christy was relaxed and didn't seem in a hurry to end the session as conversation drifted into personal issues.

"Did you attend ASU?"

"I was born in Phoenix," replied Bob, "but as a teenager I went to live with my uncle's family in Philadelphia. I attended Temple University for a degree in law enforcement. Then I did a stint in the Army as an MP. Afterward, I took more courses at ASU to be able to acquire my PI license."

"Married? Divorced?"

He shook his head. "Neither one. You?"

"Almost, but no." She looked away and shifted her position. "I spent all my years in Scottsdale, except for my time at U of A in Tucson."

"So now you're at Scottsdale PD."

"Yep. Detective Division."

"And now you're my favorite cop."

She scowled. "I told you, I'm a detective."

"Sorry, my favorite detective."

A smile returned. "You're kind of goofy, but I like you. Coffee's not bad either."

Bob was happy a friendship seemed to blossom. On finishing the coffee, she turned and walked to the door. Bob asked if he could see her again, to which she grinned and said, "Maybe." Her radio barked as she walked out and closed the door.

CHAPTER 5

LAURA AT BOB'S OFFICE

Confidential Investigations was located in a two-story office building just west of downtown Scottsdale. An insurance broker and an advertising agency occupied the first floor. On the second floor was the Silk Parlor, a party service owned by Gina Rossi, and at the other end of the hall was Confidential Investigations.

The office of Confidential Investigations had an outer secretarial office and an inner private office. Through a side door near Bob's desk was a restroom with shower, and beyond that a narrow room outfitted as a crash pad with a bed, chair, dresser and closet. The office with the partial apartment had been grandfathered in when the building was sold and renovated several years ago.

Sunday morning Bob went to the Dunkin' Donuts drive-through window, ordered a large coffee as well as an egg, ham and cheese on English muffin and arrived at his office at 8:20. He liked being at his desk early and weekends were no exception.

He walked through the empty outer office where a few weeks ago, a pretty secretary had sat. Business being slow, and a desire for a raise, had motivated her to leave for greener pastures. Maybe, he thought, he could hire a high school senior to at least put some order into his filing system and answer the phone. He hoped that being able to read efficiently and to speak intelligently wasn't asking too much of a high school student these days.

He unlocked and entered the inner office and turned on the TV before sitting at his large 1940s era mahogany desk obtained at an estate sale and refurbished. Bob watched TV news while he ate his Dunkin' Donuts breakfast. His interest was piqued on hearing news of the murder of the man named Jack Harvey in his bombed out car. Why was he killed, he wondered? Was it a mob hit, a bad drug deal, or maybe an irate ex-spouse?

Bob thought about calling Gina, as he hadn't heard from her in a couple weeks. He sure hated to miss out on any of her parties. He knew Gina from when she established the Silk Parlor in the building several years ago and had often been invited to the parties. Gina had a string of beautiful women that she employed as hostesses when a party or celebration was being catered. Her clientele were limited to select high rollers. The women employed were high-end models that Gina had brought in from LV and LA.

Bob had been immediately attracted to Laura, a beautiful woman and personal friend of Gina's from LA. Gina had asked Bob not to get involved with her, as she wanted Laura to be engaging and attentive to her male guests. Bob respected Gina and thus did as she asked. Laura was the leading hostess in Gina's retinue. On her own time, she commanded top fee for her companionship. She was currently living in a small apartment in Scottsdale and had been with Gina for almost a year. Gina had told Bob that much of Laura's money went to support her father in an Alzheimer's nursing home in Illinois.

Bob received a call from Gina mid-morning.

"Gina, how've you been? You need a handsome single male at your party?"

She chuckled. "Bob, listen. My dear friend Laura might have inadvertently gotten into trouble Saturday afternoon."

Bob assumed a serious tone. "Tell me."

"I thought before she or I become overly alarmed, she could talk to you and get your opinion and suggestion of what to do to avoid further complications."

"Sure. What happened?"

"I should have called earlier. I'd like Laura to give you the details. Can I send her right over?"

"Of course."

"Thank you, Bob." She hung up.

When the knock came on the outer door, Bob hurried to unlock it and welcome Laura into his office. The strikingly beautiful woman had infatuated him during previous encounters at the Silk Parlor. Laura wasn't smiling as she came into the office with a large bag on a shoulder strap. She said she was worried and frightened by what her experience Saturday afternoon might mean for her safety. He had to concentrate on their conversation, as he couldn't help the distraction of admiring her. As he listened to what she had to say, he too became alarmed.

"You're mainly concerned about the two men in the hallway…that came out of Carmine's room?"

She spoke calmly but Bob noticed she kept wringing her hands. "They knew I saw them come out of that room. They stopped and turned toward me. They wore masks – the kind that looks so real. They were identical. It frightened me and I was just about to run back the way I came, when just then several hotel guests started down the hall behind me laughing and being boisterous."

"That scared them off?"

She nodded. "But those men saw me; maybe know who I am by now."

"Maybe. Lets back up a little first. The TV news last night said Carmine had been murdered. Do you have any idea why Carmine was hit?"

She frowned. "He said things…you know."

Bob cleared his throat. "Pillow talk… is that going to be a problem for you now?"

"Gina and I talked a lot." Laura paused. "We think he never allowed anyone to do drug business for the outfit. He threatened to remove anyone of his crew involved in the drug trade."

"Remove…?"

She shrugged. "He could be harsh."

"Last year he ceded operational control of the outfit to his nephew Frank," said Bob. "I imagine Frank may have a different view when it comes to drug sales."

"That bothered Carmine. But he could no longer stop it."

"Carmine had enemies. Didn't he?"

"I'm sure. I don't know how, but recently he became aware of a federal grand jury investigation into the outfit's operations in Arizona. He was incensed. He hinted that someone was going to pay dearly for betraying the family. He found out that a grand jury in Chicago was also considering indictments of several Palumbo associates."

"Was he afraid of being targeted…killed?"

"Carmine said he had no choice, now, but to remove any threat to him or the organization, even if they were family."

"Wow. Didn't it make you a little scared to learn so much from him?"

"He treated me very nice and was very generous. But he did say, more than once, to keep what I saw and heard to myself. I quickly agreed, but maybe I had already heard too much."

"How did you actually hear about Carmine's murder? From Gina?"

"Yes, as soon as I arrived at the Silk Parlor. She told me about the car explosion, also."

"Yeah, that woke me up. Heard there was a guy in it when it blew."

Laura shook her head. "Dreadful…"

"Have you talked to the police?"

"Not yet. Afraid to. I expect by now they know I was there. There are cameras there and the bartender knows I see Carmine just about every week. They'll be looking for me."

"Are you worried about the police?"

"Somewhat. With police attention and publicity, I have to worry about what Carmine's people would do to me if they became suspicious and thought I was involved."

"Have you met his nephew, Frank?"

She shook her head. "I know Carmine thought a lot of him. He said he was tough but had more sense than anyone else in the outfit. But I'm afraid of him, of what he would do if he thought I had anything to do with his uncle's murder."

"But we know it was the two guys you saw coming out of the room. No one can say you had anything to do with it."

"Even so, they saw me. They must know who I am by now. It terrifies me. They'll find me."

"You are in a risky situation. By sheer luck, they didn't kill you when they saw you, but they will for sure be looking for you. That was Friday afternoon. This is Sunday. I think you have to disappear for a while. Hopefully the law will soon arrest them or someone from the outfit will take them out."

Laura looked down at her lap and was silent.

"I wonder whether the two men were renegades in the Palumbo outfit," said Bob, "or were they members of the rival outfit from Chicago, the Rinaldi people."

Laura looked at Bob and shook her head. He saw what he thought was a profound sadness overwhelming her. He knew he had to help her.

Bob had concluded some insurance investigation business over a year earlier in Frank Palumbo's favor. He had saved him from a personal injury lawsuit by a medically handicapped car driver involved in a collision. Frank had expressed his appreciation at the time and suggested someday he would return the favor. Bob was not at ease, however, in this relationship. He knew Frank had been a made-man in the old Palumbo organization with a tough reputation. Now he wondered what sort of ruse he could use with Frank to glean information of Carmine's murder. He didn't want Frank to become suspicious of him from such an inquiry.

Bob knew some of the history of the Palumbo family and he thought about it now. Carmine Palumbo, 76, retired mob boss from Chicago, lived part of the year in Arizona and had just been murdered. His brother, Mike Palumbo, the previous Palumbo boss of the Chicago outfit, had been murdered two years earlier in Chicago at age 72. Frank Palumbo, 36, nephew of Carmine and son of Mike, had been overheard by a news reporter in a crowded bar expressing suspicion that his own life and that of his son, Alfredo, might well be in danger in the coming struggle for control of the remnants of the Palumbo organization. Additionally, the FBI and IRS waged continuous harassment of the outfit in their attempt to acquire prosecutable evidence of racketeering, money laundering, tax evasion and murder. The existence of a federal grand jury investigation had leaked out.

Bob asked Laura to bear with him while he called Frank and felt him out. Laura grimaced and then nodded. Bob phoned Frank and left a message. Frank returned the call a few minutes later.

"This is Frank. You called?"

"I did. How are you these days?"

"Alright. What's up?"

"I just wanted to extend my sympathy on the death of your uncle. It's a tragic thing."

"Carmine didn't just die. He was fuckin' murdered."

"Jesus, Frank. Who would do this? Cops have any suspects?"

"Cops? Forget about it."

"But why Carmine? Robbery?"

"Oh, there was a bit of cash stolen…as an after thought."

"That's terrible. I'm sorry."

"Family's in turmoil. People are on edge. Remember, my father was killed two years ago."

"Just wanted you to know, I was thinking about you."

"Thanks, Bob. Take care." He disconnected.

Laura looked at Bob. He frowned and shook his head. "I really think it would be best if you could take a trip somewhere, maybe visit friends and relatives…or just get lost."

"Why? What did he say?"

"Frank is intent on finding the person that killed his uncle. He's really upset."

"What's that mean for me?"

"I think if he heard about you being a witness, you would be the center of attention. Likely others would hear about you."

"Those two men…"

"Maybe after a few weeks those two guys would be long gone or the cops would have them, or maybe Frank's people would have killed them."

Laura slowly shook her head. "I can't be gone. Can't lose my clientele."

"Maybe for a couple weeks?"

"I can't lose my clientele." She shook her head. "I can't."

CHAPTER 6

LAURA STAYS AT BOB'S OFFICE

Laura balked at Bob's suggestion made after his conversation with Frank Palumbo.

"Bob, you know I have clients. They're special. It took me a long time to establish these relationships. If I have to hide out for a week or more, I may well lose some of them."

"But we're talking about your safety, maybe your life," said Bob. "I'm serious."

Laura nodded slowly. "I know you are. Gina said you were a good guy. But I'm fearful of losing my high-end clientele. I may just have to risk some trouble."

"Maybe lay low for a few days?"

She grimaced and retrieved her phone from her bag and called Gina.

"Hi, yes, it's Laura. I'm here with Bob. He's rather adamant that I stay here, but I don't want to risk losing my clients."

"He's making sense, Laura. Stay out of sight for a few days."

"Bob said not to stay with you as the Silk Parlor would be where they'd look first…if they were looking for me."

"I think he's right. This is where you're known from."

"He talked to Frank…Palumbo."

"Really? What did he say?"

"I guess Frank is very upset and determined to find out who killed his uncle. Bob didn't want him to know I had been there at that time…at the hotel I mean."

"That's a good thought. I imagine Frank's on a tear. It's a good reason to lay low."

"I would rather just stay over there with you for a day or two."

"Bob is making a lot of sense. Stay with him for a couple days. He's a good guy."

"I know… maybe for a day or two."

"Stay safe and call me tomorrow." Gina clicked off.

Laura put her phone back in her bag. "I guess I'll stay for a couple days. Bob, I apologize if I seem ungrateful. You're a good guy."

He smiled and she looked down at her lap.

"Laura, why don't you put your things in my studio apartment?" He indicated his small bedroom, just next to his office, with a thumb over his shoulder. "There's clean bedding and stuff in the dresser." He was quick to add, "I'll sleep out here on the couch."

She stood and looked where he had indicated. "I'm sorry for the inconvenience I'm causing you." She picked up her bag and went into the studio apartment. A few minutes later she returned and took a seat on the couch. "Bob, thank you. I really value my independence. This is hard for me. I really do need to keep with my clients."

Bob nodded. "I understand."

She smiled, "I do appreciate what you're doing for me. Gina always said you're a good person and…I…I've always liked you."

"Being an extra at Gina's parties was always fun."

Laura smiled. "Uh-huh, for me too. Nice way to meet people."

"You were always the most beautiful hostess there." Had he really said that?

Laura shifted her gaze away from him. "Thank you. You're sweet."

Bob cleared his throat. "Gina didn't want me to make a pass at you."

She looked at him seemingly surprised. "I…she never said anything."

"I don't think she wanted me to distract you – you had your dad to look after."

She nodded, but it was several seconds before she responded. "Gina is a friend… I did bring in quite a bit of money…" She seemed to lose her thought.

"I guess Carmine was rather important to you?" Did he dare go there?

She didn't look at him. "He was very generous, treated me well."

"He had enemies."

"I don't know why… retired. It's just too sad."

"I'm sorry." He paused. "I know he wasn't in the business anymore."

She looked at him. "Not day to day. He just wanted to be left in peace."

"He put it all in his nephew's hands."

"Uh-huh, he spoke well of Frank. I never really met him. You did?"

"Yes. I did some insurance work in his favor a few years back. We got along alright."

"Carmine worried whether Frank could keep the outfit together. He was on the phone with him often."

"There's going to be a lot of police inquiry into the assassination. They'll soon learn that you were a witness."

"I really only saw…they had masks…"

"Even so, the killers might want to do you harm. It would be best if you were hard to find for a few days."

"I appreciate what you're saying – really, I do. It's that I worked so hard to get these clients. They're safe and high rollers. I stand to lose a lot."

"Laura, I worry about you losing your life."

She nodded and looked at her clenched hands. "Thank you. I know you do."

Laura avoided further conversation about her clients or her relationship with Carmine. She seemed eager to talk of her early years and Bob reciprocated, enjoying her company. Bob had pizza delivered. They became at ease with each other, and Bob was happy that she was there with him. The two of them watched TV but saw no updates on the murder of Carmine. Before they retired, Laura told Bob she wanted to go home the next day; emphasizing her need to keep the relationship she had with her clients. Bob asked her to wait another day. But when she resisted, he hesitantly agreed not to make an issue of it, but he was saddened and fearful of the idea. He was afraid that the two killers would be looking for her.

Before falling asleep, Bob ruminated about Frank. He wondered if Frank, though maybe not directly involved in his uncle's murder, might well benefit from his demise. Bob realized if Frank were formally elected as head of the family, he would be in a position to exert control without interference by anyone. He wondered if Frank would consider Laura as a threat to him from her intimate familiarity with Carmine. Could she pose a risk to him in an eventual grand jury inquiry? Bob wasn't convinced Laura was really safe staying there with him, but maybe for a few days. Even though he had a gun in the office, could he really protect her if hit men broke in? What about later? A week? A month? He would try again in the morning to change her mind.

CHAPTER 7

TRAGEDY

Monday morning Laura listened to Bob as they finished their coffee. He tried once more to get her to stay another day.

"It's just to let things cool down a little. Hopefully the two killers will have skipped town."

Laura shook her head slowly. "I thought about it over night and I made up my mind. I have to leave…get ready for tonight. I'm truly grateful for your concern and putting me up last night."

When she got up to leave she hugged and kissed him. "Thanks for everything."

Then she picked up her big shoulder bag and left without another word. Laura drove to her apartment and parked angled to the curb in front of the building, as she usually did.

A casual bystander across the street and within two hundred feet saw a late model gray Toyota stop behind Laura's her car as she was just getting out of the vehicle. The bystander would later report to a policeman this driver to be a casually dressed white man of about five and half feet height and he got out of his car and walked quickly to Laura as she got out of her car. She heard two pops and saw Laura crumble to the ground, part way out of her car. This witness reported the Toyota drove away in an unhurried manner.

- - - -

Christy arrived a few minutes after the police taped off the area. As another detective helped look for evidence, Christy interviewed prospective witnesses. One witness, a female, had told an officer about the late model gray Toyota and of seeing only one medium-size man get out of the car, the shooter. A uniformed officer reported to Christy that he had interviewed another female witness who had been walking on the opposite side of the street. She claimed she saw what she thought was a gray Toyota with an Arizona license plate containing 62 as the last two digits, pulling away from behind Laura's car. She said she had heard two clear pop sounds.

Christy walked both sides of the street looking for video cameras that a resident may have hopefully installed at their window. But she didn't see any.

A policeman found two spent shell cases for a .22 caliber pistol lying under her car. A blue tarp was draped over the deceased to offer a measure of respect and to hide the sight from bystanders.

- - - -

Bob heard a short news flash of a shooting on the police scanner Monday morning while sitting at his desk. The victim was not identified, but Bob was overwhelmed with panic and fear. He left his office and rushed to his car to drive to where Laura had said she lived.

He had to park a half block away due to the yellow tape and the many police vehicles. Bob, now full of dread, rushed to where he saw a blue tarp covering the deceased. In a panic and unmindful of the situation, he rushed to identify the body. He heard policemen yell at him to get behind the yellow tape, but he had to see the victim, to be sure. He lifted the corner of the blue tarp and saw Laura lying part way out of her car, her head covered in blood.

Two policemen grabbed him and forcibly dragged him beyond the yellow tape barrier and warned him that he would be arrested if he tried to enter the restricted area again. EMTs stood by helplessly. The bloody sight had stirred a rage in Bob and he now struggled with the bile rising in his throat.

- - - -

Christy stood about twenty yards from where Laura laid while she took photos. She noticed Bob's arrival. His defiant presence and disregard for the yellow tape barrier angered her. She went to him and began to berate him for his poor judgment.

"What the hell's the matter with you? You know better." She shook her head. "Are you trying to get arrested? Why are you here, anyway?"

"Laura was staying at my office yesterday and last night…to be safe from repercussions."

Christy grimaced. "What the heck are you talking about?"

Bob wiped at his face with his hand. "She had seen the two shooters of Carmine Palumbo."

Christy's anger dissipated somewhat as she looked at him. "I want to hear more about what Laura said to you. I'll look you up later, but in the meantime you are to stay behind the yellow tape or better yet, go home. You can't do any good here."

Bob looked at the blue tarp and nodded, but didn't move away.

Her voice softened. "Bob, you don't look well. You're pale and perspiring. Let the EMTs take a look at you."

"No." He started walking toward his car.

Christy wasn't angry any longer, instead felt a sense of pity as she realized Bob had known the victim.

When Bob got to his car, his mouth filled with saliva and he suddenly had to vomit. He sat in his car for ten minutes with the air conditioner on 'high' to calm himself. The cup holder held some day-old coffee.

It helped Bob sooth his throat and chase the bad taste from his mouth as he drove home.

On reaching his apartment he turned on the TV to catch any updates of the murder. However, unable to focus on anything, he just paced around the floor. Then, upset and angry, he made some fresh coffee and chewed on cold leftover pizza. On feeling the rise of bile, he tossed the pizza away and sat quietly at the table sipping coffee, feeling sick and upset. He felt the pangs of guilt and failure. Unable to concentrate on anything, he laid his head on his arm and closed his eyes.

CHAPTER 8
CHRISTY STOPS BY

Bob awakened to knocking on the apartment door. He looked at the clock and was surprised at how late it had become. It was almost 6pm. He had fallen asleep on the table with his head on his arm. He rubbed the knotted muscles in his neck and sore arm as he stood up. There was another knock on the door, more insistent.

Bob opened the door and saw Christy standing there, a worried look on her face. He stared at her, at a loss for words for a few seconds.

"Are you going to invite me in, or what?"

He apologized and stood aside so she could enter. He closed the door behind her, shutting off the hot afternoon air.

"You look like shit."

"Sorry…"

"Look, Bob, I got worried about you. You didn't look well earlier. You said something about Laura having been here with you?"

"Seeing her like that… I got sick and in a helpless rage… Went back to my car, but I couldn't hold it down…just got sick…so damn angry."

"I'm sorry. It was a dreadful thing that happened."

"Did you learn who did this…this crime?"

She shook her head. "I hope to hear whatever you can add to my investigation of this murder." She paused. "Bob, I know about her and Carmine Palumbo. I talked to Gina Rossi. I searched for video cameras

Treachery | 29

along that street, but there weren't any. I checked on my computer for your home address. It might be useful for me to know what Laura told you of her relationship with Carmine."

"No one saw anything?"

"A witness observed a car leave the immediate area and memorized part of the license number. Detectives and patrol officers will be chasing down this lead. Meanwhile, an area canvas is being conducted."

"I tried to talk her out of leaving here…knew it would be dangerous for her."

"Think we can sit down at the table? I'd like to go over what you remember of the conversation with Laura; see if any clues have been overlooked."

Christy sat facing Bob. "You look pale. You going to be all right?"

He nodded.

Christy coaxed Bob to tell her what he had surmised in talking with Laura. He briefly described their conversation about Carmine and his nephew. But she lost his attention, as he seemed to retreat inward.

After a few minutes, where Bob was not being talkative, Christy stood up and asked where the coffee cups were.

He pointed to a cupboard next to the sink.

She took one and poured herself a cup and topped off Bob's. Reaching into the refrigerator she took out a carton of milk and whitened her coffee and then Bob's.

"Bob…you look pale and sweaty. Are you going to be all right?"

He slowly shook his head and asked Christy to give him a few minutes. Christy was unsuccessful in reengaging Bob in a fruitful conversation about Laura. Bob was not drinking his coffee. She saw that he had another bead of perspiration forming on his brow. She stood up and went to him.

"Bob. Stand up. Come on, you're not looking well." Her voice was insistent.

Christy coaxed and guided him into his bedroom. Then, she reached over the bed and pulled the covers down part way and told him to lie down. She pulled off his loafers and dropped them on the floor. She reached to loosen his belt over his objections, and then pulled the cover over him.

His reaction to the murder of Laura had surprised her, and now she felt herself drawn to him. She touched his brow and felt the wetness but didn't think he had a fever. Christy told him to go to sleep for a while; that she would finish her coffee and leave. She told him she would stop by his office tomorrow some time, and they could finish their talk. She ruffled his hair and told him to "Get some sleep."

She noticed the shoulder-holstered pistol on a chair back, and decided she could ask him about it the next time she saw him. Despite her cautionary instincts, she couldn't help the attraction she felt for him. He was no youngster that was obvious to her, but thought even if he was somewhat older than she; he might be a caring and sensitive man. She mused it would certainly be different than her recent experiences.

CHAPTER 9
FRAUD SUSPECT

Bob woke up early the next morning, removed his rumpled and sweaty clothes and tossed them in the laundry basket. He felt some embarrassment on thinking of his distress the previous day and of Christy trying to help him. A hot shower felt good and he luxuriated in it for ten minutes. Finally, he dried off and finished his toiletries. He put on clean clothes and headed for Dunkin Donuts on the way to his office. The thought of Laura, murdered, haunted him.

It was 9:40 when Bob finished his morning coffee and blueberry muffin at his desk. He had time to consider the clandestine visitations he had to make to each fraud suspect. He always hoped to get photographic evidence. This was best done at night for his own safety, although exceptions had to be made. State agency's solicited his help in gathering evidence against unemployment insurance and welfare cheats. Insurance companies often solicited help to investigate claims of workplace injury or peculiar circumstances in automobile accident injury. Bob had needed to hire part time help as his business grew.

The previous week, Bob had received a call from Lori Beckman of the Industrial Commission of Arizona. She had talked about investigating a claimant, Rick Greene, suspected of Workers Comp fraud, pursuant to a purported warehouse accident that had left the claimant to report severe back pain. A doctor who had examined the worker supported the claim. According to Lori Beckman this claimant had been involved in two dubious claims in the past three years.

Investigating auto insurance fraud, unemployment insurance fraud, health insurance fraud, and Workers Comp fraud provided Bob with steady income. Occasionally, he landed a private investigative contract that fattened the coffers. Several weeks ago, Bob had been asked by the law office of Morgan and Dunlop to investigate whether Rick Greene had a steady job that would allow successful litigation for back child support. Apparently Greene was over six months in arrears. Bob's office was following up on this request as part of their rounds of surveillance.

Bob pushed the call button on his cell phone for Greg Auburn, the college dropout he employed part time for clandestine investigations. Greg was good with a camera and patient to obtain the evidence needed. One in four subjects during the past year had proven to be cheating the Workers Comp program, a twenty-five percent increase over the year before.

"Hi Greg, what are you up to?"

"Just finished a load of laundry. I'll be going out on my rounds in a couple hours. You need something?"

"I received a call from Morgan and Dunlop about their interest in Rick Greene."

"Rick Greene? I have him on my list of bad boys to check on when I go out. What's a law office want with him?"

"It seems Greene is six months in arrears with his child support. They want to go after him if he has a steady job that would allow successful litigation. I told them we could investigate and let them know."

"So this Greene character is an all around fraudster, huh?"

"Sounds like it. Listen, Greg. I need you to be cautious with this guy. He's a know criminal in the Palumbo gang…a real badass."

"Okay. I'll try to not let him know I'm looking at him."

"Spend some time in the next few nights checking on the voracity of his Workers Comp claim and see if he's employed somewhere."

"I've got three others on my list that I'm looking at."

"I know. Stay safe."

- - - -

It was 5:30 in the afternoon when Bob heard a knock at the office door. He had forgotten to unlock the door that morning. When he opened the door Christy greeted him with a smile.

"Detective, this is a surprise. I'm happy to see you." His heart rate increased.

"Oh, I'm done for the day. Thought I'd come by and see if you're okay. You didn't look so good yesterday."

"Thanks. I guess I needed some sleep. It was a terrible thing what happened to Laura."

"Yes, it was. You knew her…"

"Yes. Never got to know her well but like I told you, she had stayed in my office that night. She was a good person."

"That's what Gina said."

"Is there news regarding the murder?"

"The only thing we have is a partial license plate of a gray Nissan. Phoenix PD found the license plate lying on the side of the road near the zoo."

"But not the car?"

She shook her head. "The plate had been wiped clean. It had been stolen that morning from a car in the Wal-Mart parking lot in east Mesa."

"Someone did some planning."

"Uh-huh. No clues to pursue at this time, but I have a couple detectives still canvassing."

"And there's nothing new about the murder in the hotel?" asked Bob.

Christy shook her head. "We're analyzing the video camera images taken in the hallway by Carmine's hotel room. Also, we're looking at images of the two purported hit men from the hotel entrance showing them coming and going. Unfortunately, the two men were wearing full and identical facial masks."

"No identifying features?"

"Not yet. The recording is being further processed at our Forensic Sciences Lab. I don't have a lot of hope."

Bob shook his head. "It's upsetting."

"I know. I'll talk to you tomorrow. Hopefully, I'll know more."

Bob watched her leave and didn't try to dissuade her. He had been surprised at her visit. She surely had a lot to do and could have just called, he thought. He wanted to see more of her and wondered if it would be possible.

- - - -

Greg was spying on Rick Greene at the end of the day trying to gather evidence of Workers Comp violation for a supposed back injury. He had followed Greene when he left his house to go to Tony's, a well-known mob bar in north Phoenix. He remembered Bob's warning about Greene as he kept an eye on the bar and glanced frequently at the rearview mirror. A high-grade Minolta camera with a telephoto lens attachment served Greg well to observe and record the activity in the side parking area of the bar. He was able to just make out the license number on the big Buick.

Rick Greene helped an unknown man bring out a rolled up rug and Greg watched as they both struggled to lift it into the trunk of the car. Greene then went back inside the bar. Greg took many time-stamped photos with the digital camera. Pictures included the license number of the car as well as the lighted sign for Tony's bar. Greg wondered if a body was wrapped in the rug from the awkward way the two men handled it. He shook his head, I'm watching too many late night movies. It was obvious that Rick Greene didn't suffer from a back injury as had been reported to Workers Comp.

When the Buick left, driven by the unknown man, another car also left from the other side of the building and disappeared in the opposite direction from that of the Buick. Greg was not able to get a photo of the other vehicle and had not seen who was in it. He wondered if it had been Greene. Several minutes later he stopped at a convenience store for a snack. He called Bob to check in.

"Greg, I worry about you getting hurt one of these days."

"Yeah. You might have to give me a bonus." He unwrapped the cellophane around a pastry.

"Seriously, Greene is a nasty bastard."

"I hear you." He took a big bite of the pastry.

"So you think you nailed Greene for Workers Comp?"

"I did. Got good pictures with this Minolta. He's certainly not suffering from any back injuries."

"You're not still there are you?" Bob sounded worried.

"No, I left. I'm at a Seven Eleven. I'm sending you an email right now with the pictures."

"Okay. Great."

"By the way, I saw Greene help an unknown man bring out a rolled up rug and put it in the trunk of the Buick."

"No kidding? Like in the movies?"

"It sure looked like there was a body in the rug. Check the photos and you'll see what I mean."

"Where did Greene go?"

"When the Buick drove off, Greene went back into the bar. However, I think he left by another door because a car left by that other side very shortly after the Buick drove off. But I have no proof of that."

"Greg, get your ass back here. I sure hope you weren't spotted."

"Okay. I'm headed back." He stuffed the remains of the pastry into his mouth and started the car.

CHAPTER 10
PALUMBO SUSPECTS

Bob hadn't slept well that night, awakened several times to the thought of Laura and the scene of her murder. Out of bed, angry and depressed, he sat at his computer and prepared a Letter-to-the-Editor to email to the Valley Gazette in Phoenix. He hoped it would be in the next day's paper.

Assassinated

A few days ago, a beautiful friend had the misfortune to witness two men leaving the hotel room of a prominent person. Inside the room, the man was found dead. My friend clearly saw the two hit men, but was saved from her own demise by the sudden appearance of several hotel guests. However, two days later she was assassinated in front of her apartment. The killers had eliminated the only person able to link them to the deceased man in the hotel room, or so they thought.

Her story was told first hand to several people and now the quest to identify, arrest and prosecute these killers is top-most on the minds of those wanting justice for this beautiful life cut short. RW

After he sent the email to the newspaper, Bob took a shower and readied himself for the day. Arriving at his office that Thursday morning, he ate his customary blueberry muffin and coffee, and then sent an email to Christy. In the message he outlined Greg's observations and attached the most interesting of the photos. He asked Christy if she recognized the man helping with the rug, and mentioned the one wearing a baseball hat was his subject, Rick Greene. He asked her to trace the license number of the Buick.

An hour later, Christy called him. "Hi Bob got your email. The registration on that Buick is to a Mark Bianchi."

"Thanks for checking on it. Who is he?"

"He's thirty two and a low level soldier in the Palumbo organization. He's had several arrests in Arizona but no convictions."

"How about the guy with Greene?"

"We couldn't make an identification of the guy helping Greene. Just wasn't clear enough. It's an interesting photo, I'll hold onto that one."

Bob chuckled, "That Greene guy is obviously faking his injury. I'll issue a report to the Industrial Commission, Workers Comp, suggesting Greene is faking his injury. I'll send my photo evidence but without any conclusion of criminal activity."

"Can you hold off for another day? I need to give time for one of our detectives to follow up on this incident with the Phoenix PD."

"Sure. Another day won't hurt."

"Okay. Thanks. Catch you later."

It was four o'clock when Bob received another call from Christy. "Hello Bob. Little while ago I heard from one of our detectives that the man driving the Buick, Mark Bianchi, was found dead in his car of a gunshot at an intersection near his Phoenix home."

"No kidding? Wow."

"There's more. In the trunk of the Buick they found the body of Victor Diego, a thirty-year-old soldier for the Rinaldi family. He was suspected in the murder of Angelo Palumbo, nephew of Carmine and brother of Frank Palumbo. This Angelo guy was killed two years ago at age 32 in a suspicious auto accident in Los Angeles."

"Geez, you need a score sheet to keep everyone straight."

"Bob, I'll be leaving work shortly. Think you'd be interested in joining me for a pizza?"

"You bet. Been thinking about you a lot." His heartbeat quickened.

"Well, I like that. I'm thinking of a small quiet place, Ricardo's, in east Phoenix. It's just north of McDowell Road at 44th Street. I can be there just after six."

"Six works for me. See you then."

Bob prepared a report to send in a couple days to Lori Beckman at the Industrial Commission detailing the outcome of the investigation of Rick Greene.

CHAPTER 11

RICARDO'S PIZZA

Ricardo's Pizza, a small shop in a strip mall in northeast Phoenix had been there for over ten years. An older couple and their daughter owned the shop since Grandfather Ricardo passed away two years ago. Christy had stopped there initially several years past on her way home from visiting her mother in a nearby nursing home. Hodgkin's disease and dementia were taking a toll on the elderly woman. Christy visited often.

Christy spotted Bob as he walked in, and waved from a booth at the back of the store. It felt good to see him as he approached her with a smile. He looked well dressed in button down shirt, tie and blue blazer. She appreciated that he had obviously shaved before going to meet her. But, she wondered if he would get her in trouble with his quest to avenge the murder of Laura. They talked briefly about the lack of real progress in the investigation of Laura's murder. Christy wanted to go over what Greg had witnessed at Tony's. She suggested ordering a large thin-crust pizza with a variety of toppings to which Bob smiled and nodded. Christy asked for a diet soda and Bob a beer.

They talked more about the investigation that Bob and Greg had successfully done of Rick Greene, and Christy said her office would examine the photographic evidence and give it to the DA.

When Bob told her of the Letter-to-the-Editor he had sent to the Phoenix paper that morning, she was surprised.

"Really? What motivated you to do that?" Her face clouded.

"I can't get this out of my mind. It's so sad, what happened. I get so angry."

"You're taking this maybe too personally?"

Bob nodded slowly. "I feel guilty. I should have somehow convinced her stay with me."

Christy grimaced and nodded. "I understand. It was horrible…and you knew her. I'm sorry. I hope we can identify her killers soon and get them locked up."

"Do you think the FBI can provide assistance in identifying the masked hit men?"

She scowled. "I'm not keen on asking the FBI for help yet. As long as we think the killers are still in the area, I'm sure our officers can handle the situation. Also, I'm afraid when the FBI gets involved, it will no longer be our case."

She saw the irritation with her reasoning in Bob's grimace but he didn't press the issue and she kept up conversation with small talk. She mentioned her mother was not going to improve with Hodgkin's and dementia and that it saddened her. Also, her father had passed away several years earlier. When Bob asked, she said she had been raised in Scottsdale and had gone to the University of Arizona to graduate with a BS and Masters in Criminology and Criminal Justice.

Christy's phone buzzed. "I'm sorry." She looked at a text message then at Bob. "A newspaper reporter from the Valley Gazette and his car has been reported missing. It's been twenty-four hours."

Bob frowned. "That doesn't bode well. Who is it?"

"Walter Schneider. He's been investigating Palumbo activities for several years in the Phoenix area, as well as in Las Vegas. He's well known to the Palumbo family."

Christy sent a text reply and turned back to Bob. "Hate to think of what may have happened to him."

She saw him scowl and guessed what was coming. "Have you heard anything at all about the Laura murder?"

Christy felt his sadness and shook her head. "No new leads on her murder or that of Carmine. But as you have said, they are no doubt related. I have to place Frank Palumbo high on my list of suspects."

Bob nodded slowly. "Nothing on the gray Toyota?"

"No. I told you they found the stolen license plate along the edge of the road where someone tossed it."

"How about the video cameras at the hotel? You said there were some useful images."

"The images are fairly good, but the shooters were wearing identical full facial masks. The images are now at the Forensic Science Lab for additional processing."

Bob shook his head slowly. "I can't stand to think that no one will be prosecuted for this."

Christy frowned. "Give it a little time. We will pursue every clue we get."

Bob nodded. "Laura said the two men coming out of Carmine's room would probably have killed her right then, except for the sudden appearance of a group of people."

"I know. She was a witness and a little too close for them to let her live."

"I have to wonder whether it's the same guys responsible for the murder of Jack Harvey with the car bomb. And now, we have Walter Schneider missing."

"You're suggesting it was the work of Palumbo people?"

Bob shrugged.

"It's a bit of a stretch. If the Carmine hit wasn't by a Palumbo person, it could be someone we haven't thought of," said Christy. "The bombings could be Palumbo's work."

"Anything new with the Harvey bombing?" asked Bob.

"We have a couple detectives working it. Harvey was a known Palumbo financial guy apparently having an affair with an FBI agent. One can be sure the outfit would take a dim view of that."

"Got to wonder about the reporter…was he too close?"

She shrugged. "Personally, I'm going to concentrate on identifying the two creeps that killed Carmine."

"And Laura," Bob was quick to add.

"Yep."

"Do you have to go back to the office this evening?" Where had that surge of boldness come from?

Christy grinned. "No, but I'll be calling in for an update."

Bob was silent for a moment before saying, "I'm happy we got together."

She smiled. "I did want to know more about you…and I like your company."

They ordered wine and a specialty Italian desert.

Later, when they were standing next to her car, she came up to him and wrapped her arms around his waist and placed her head against his shoulder. "I like you."

He held her close for a few seconds and then on impulse tilted her head up slightly and kissed her.

The kiss lasted for a second before she gently pushed him away. "I enjoyed our time together and I'd like to do it again."

"Me, too."

She got into her car.

Bob drove home with his heart beating rapidly. The attraction he felt for Christy was more than arousing, he enjoyed being in her company.

CHAPTER 12
REPORTER'S DEMISE

Bob stepped away from his desk at 11 o'clock, ready to leave his office for lunch. As he pointed the remote control toward the TV, a news flash came on the screen. A loud explosion had been reported that morning in east Mesa at a large townhouse complex adjacent to a nine-hole golf course, whose early players called 9-1-1.

The news report described how the Mesa police investigated a barely recognizable Chevrolet sedan in the rear of a parking lot completely demolished by what looked like the result of two bombs. The EMT team determined there were remains of a person in the twisted and burned out vehicle. The medical examiner soon declared it was the body of a male. A detective had queried the dispatcher as to the identity of the owner, based on the license plate number. The name had come back as being the missing Walter Schneider, a famous crime reporter at the Valley Gazette based in Phoenix and known for his dedicated investigation of Palumbo and other crime businesses and activities.

Bob called Christy and asked if she could give him any more details. She declined and said she'd know more at the end of the day. He turned off the TV and left the office. He walked a few blocks to a small sandwich shop nearer the center of town and sat outside under a shade umbrella. He enjoyed watching the lunch crowd that walked by, especially the attractive office and sales ladies in the fashion district. He was reminded that he had lost his secretary a few weeks ago, and that maybe he should think about hiring another. He enjoyed a generous Rueben sandwich with a cold beer and toyed with the idea of going for another beer. Duty calls he told himself.

He placed some bills under the beer glass and headed back to his office taking a short cut to a service alley behind the restaurant. He soon heard the crunch of shoes on the rough pavement behind him. Just as his senses alarmed him, he turned. Two casually dressed men suddenly accosted him. His attempt to fight back was hampered by the grip of the larger man who clamped his arms to his sides. The shorter man inflicted sudden and bruising blows to his abdomen. Bob's attempt to kick at the man was futile as nausea and pain overwhelmed him.

The assault was short lived. The men suddenly hurried away on hearing several women shouting as they came nearer. As the men left, one warned Bob, "Mind your own damn business buddy before you really get hurt."

Bob, confused, leaned on a trash dumpster for support as he fought back nausea. One woman said she had called 9-1-1. He told her thanks, but that he just wanted to go back to his office. But as he started to continue his way to the end of the alley, a police cruiser blocked his way.

An officer stepped out of the car and approached him. "Sir, do you need medical attention?"

Bob shook his head. "I'll be okay. A couple of guys thumping on me."

"They rob you?"

"No. The ladies came by and the bastards took off."

The officer was making some notes in a small notebook. "What's your name, sir?"

"Bob Wagner."

"You recognize these guys? What did they look like?"

"White guys. Tall guy and a shorter heavy guy."

"Want to make out a complaint?"

Bob shook his head. "No. Just want to go back to my office."

"Where is your office?"

"Over on the next block. Confidential Investigations."

The officer made a few more notes and shoved the notebook back into his breast pocket.

"You going to be okay, sir? You sure?"

"Yes. Thanks."

The officer went to his car and drove slowly away. Bob walked to his office not sure what the warning was about. He wondered if his making inquiries about the Carmine and Laura murders had stirred some angst with someone.

Bob took some ibuprofen at the office and washed his face. He changed his clothes as they had become soiled during the scuffle. At his desk he tried to finish reports he owed his clients; but then distracted by soreness in his ribs and face, he gave up and laid his head down on the desk and slept.

It was after five o'clock when Christy knocked on the office door. The door was unlocked and she walked in to find him asleep. When she went to him, she saw the bruises and scrapes on his face. She called his name several times before he opened his eyes. He smiled, but then winced as he sat up.

Christy had Bob tell her the whole story after which she placed a call to the Scottsdale PD. Bob went into the bathroom to freshen up. Back in the office area, he saw Christy on her cell phone in apparent exchange of text messages. She turned to Bob and said she hoped to get pictures of his assailants from video cameras behind the drugstore. Bob sat on the couch and laid his head back on the cushion.

"Why didn't you let the officer escort you back here to your office?"

"It was only to the next block."

She didn't try to hide her annoyance at his casual attitude. Christy scowled. "You forget the warning they gave you? I don't think you should be so cavalier."

He nodded and closed his eyes. "Uh-huh. I don't know what it was about."

"Those two guys could well be the same two that Laura saw at Carmine's hotel room. You said one was tall and the other short and stout."

Bob opened his eyes. "Coulda been. These guys were dressed casually, not like how Laura described them. Laura said the tall guy had been wearing a sport coat with elbow patches. The short guy had what sounded to me like a Boston Bruins jacket. Made me wonder at that time if they were from Boston."

"Sure, could be a couple of Eastern dudes. I should be getting the video photos on my phone within the hour."

Bob was fighting sleepiness as he listened to Christy.

"You want to go back to sleep…crash on your bed?"

"No. I took some ibuprofen. I'm feeling better. Besides, I have reports started that I need to send in." Bob stood up.

"How about I drive you to get some spaghetti and meatballs instead?"

Bob smiled. "That sounds good."

Just as they finished their meal, Christy's phone buzzed.

"The photos maybe?" asked Bob.

She nodded. "Lets see what they show us." She enlarged the images one at a time. "Kind of disappointing."

"It looks like the cameras were mounted high above the loading dock making the faces of these guys indistinct."

"Uh-huh. And their hats shaded their faces. I'll check with our forensics guys and see if they can enhance these images."

Bob scowled. "Don't have a lot of hope. Any news about the reporter?"

"I talked earlier to Mesa PD and the Valley Gazette and was told that Schneider had been working on a multipart series about Palumbo money laundering activities.

"I guess the Internet rumors about a federal grand jury being formed to explore crimes of Palumbo in the Phoenix area are probably true."

Christy smiled. "I've heard similar rumors but can't comment."

Bob nodded.

CHAPTER 13
NICE EVENING

On finishing their meal Christy got the waiter's attention and ordered two glasses of Chablis wine. Bob thanked her and they toasted each other.

"I enjoy being with you," said Christy smiling. "You're kind of easy to like."

"I like being with you."

"I admit I haven't been out with anyone other than my work crew in many months."

"I'm glad I met you."

"Yeah, it's kinda nice having someone to be with and share thoughts."

"Spending all my time on my business has cost me a couple of relationships," said Bob.

"I can understand that," said Christy, "from both points of view. I've never been married. Men I liked were put off by my school and work schedule."

Bob nodded a few times. "I finally hired Greg to help me part time."

"I think you need to make him permanent. He sounds like a good guy."

"He is. I think I'll offer him a permanent job instead of hiring a secretary. Things are picking up."

"That's great. Is Greg studying law enforcement?"

Treachery | 51

"No, but I'm going to suggest that he does." Bob sat back in the seat. "Thanks for dinner. I'm still sore but I feel better."

"You're looking a little better." She slid out of the booth and took his arm as they left the restaurant.

Christy pulled to a stop in front of her apartment.

Bob looked at her. "I didn't bring my car."

Christy rolled her eyes. "How about an after dinner drink?"

Bob broke into a smile and reached for the door handle.

As she unlocked the apartment door, she asked, "Do you still hurt?"

"Yes, but the meal helped a lot."

"I'm glad. Have a seat while I fix a couple drinks."

Christy placed the drink glasses on the cocktail table and settled herself against him.

He pulled her closer, and then reached for the TV remote.

Christy spoke sternly. "Put it down."

Bob was slow to grab the significance of her request.

Suddenly she pulled his head toward her and her mouth covered his.

They fumbled with each other's clothes as their passion urged them frantically onward.

Christy awoke before Bob in the early morning. She looked at him, smiled, and was glad she had finally succumbed to her desire. Thirty minutes later she had finished dressing. In the kitchen, she started the coffee maker and then went to awaken Bob. He wasn't in any hurry to get up but Christy insisted, as she had to be at her desk in less than an hour. They both gulped their coffee. Christy drove Bob to his apartment, kissed him, and then rushed to her job at the Scottsdale PD.

CHAPTER 14
NEW DEVELOPMENTS

Bob picked up the phone. "Hello. Confidential Investigations."

"Bob Wagner? This is Frank Palumbo."

"Good morning." Bob was surprised to hear from him. "What can I do for you?"

"I'll come right to the point. I've been informed you have a rather friendly relationship with a Scottsdale detective. In view of our past business and my current problems, I'd like to hear from you that this relationship is not something that will become a problem for me."

"Frank, I like this person. I got to know her when the car blew up next to my apartment. We're in a similar line of work. Neither one of us reveals confidences of what we do."

"So, you're saying what? That I shouldn't be worried?"

"Frank, I understand your concern, but my relationship with this person is not a threat to you."

"I'm certainly glad to hear you say that. I will keep that in mind."

Frank clicked off.

Bob put the phone down. Is Frank worried that I would compromise him somehow? Did it mean he was involved in the two bombings? He must have read the letter-to-the- editor…he probably figures I would help the PD with anything I learned. Maybe Frank is involved in these killings, but Carmine and Laura? I can't see that.

- - - -

The next night Greg Auburn was on stakeout within sight of a subject's residence, a small frame and stucco house in north Phoenix. The subject, Alfred Dominic, had been released on bail on a fraud charge brought by an insurance company in regard to suspicious fire damage to one of his heavily insured rental properties. Just after 10pm, Greg watched as four expensive cars drove up to the North Phoenix house within minutes of each other. Seven well-dressed men quickly entered the house. Greg read and voiced the license number of each car into a small solid-state pocket recorder. He then focused on identifying the make and model of each visiting car. A few minutes later, fearing discovery, Greg left for his home and there prepared an email to Bob summarizing his observations.

- - - -

Bob still ruminated over the brief phone conversation he had yesterday with Frank Palumbo. When he received Greg's email, he sent Christy a text message with the license numbers of the four cars and asked her to send him any information that she could on the owners.

In less than an hour, she called Bob.

"Sounds like you had Greg in a risky situation tonight."

"He was sitting on this Alfred Dominic guy as he was out on bail and we didn't want him to skip."

"Well, four of the guys he observed were likely high-ranking members of the Palumbo outfit, here from Chicago. The vehicles were rented limos from the airport."

"All here for a big get together?"

"Probably a classic sit-down among the top members of the Palumbo outfit to determine the next boss."

"So we have the Chicago guys here with Frank Palumbo?"

"That would make sense to me. Carmine is gone. I expect they'll favor to have Frank run things."

"I don't know any of the Chicago guys," said Bob.

"It would've been interesting to be a fly on the wall at that meeting."

"Wonder what the outcome was?"

"I haven't heard anything yet. But, the smart money has been on Frank. The Chicago guys are all up in years and Frank was nurtured by Carmine."

"I wonder if Frank removed any threat to his accession," said Bob.

"Well, it seems to me that Frank had the most to gain by the death of Carmine."

"Maybe. But, Frank was already running the outfit as he had been appointed by Carmine a year ago."

"Not so fast. From a practical point of view, that decision only impacted the crew here in Arizona. That's why they probably had the sit-down; to square things with the Chicago folks."

Bob agreed. "I think you're right."

"Even though I think the Rinaldi outfit would benefit by the elimination of Carmine, I have Frank high on my list of suspects. I can see where he might arrange for the killing of Carmine. Then there's the two bombings, who else but Palumbo? Of course, it's important to identify the actual gunmen and bomber."

She promised to give Bob a heads-up if she heard anything about the sit-down.

CHAPTER 15

SLEUTHING

After her shift ended the next day, Christy met Bob at the Twisted Lime lounge just south of McDowell Road in southwest Scottsdale. They relaxed and enjoyed each other's company while watching a quiz show on the TV over the bar.

Christy's phone buzzed, as they were about to leave. She looked at Bob and whispered *PD* as she put the phone to her ear. "Hello Detective."

"Christy, I was wondering if you could help me out."

"What's up, Ed?"

"I'm on foot here in Phoenix. A short guy with a Boston Red Sox t-shirt just left a smoke shop at McDowell Road and 36th Street. He got into a white Buick sedan driven by another male. Both dudes are white. They're headed east but I'm not near my car – can't follow them."

"Ed, I'm in Scottsdale. What do you need me to do?"

"I'm thinking these guys are headed your way. Can you get in a position to tail the Buick and get a plate number?"

"Well, I am just off of McDowell Road. What are you thinking? Ten minutes?"

"Yeah. Traffic's light."

"Alright. I'll give it a try."

"See ya."

Christy turned to Bob. "That was Officer Ed Merrill. He suggested a target for me to check out. There are two guys in a white Buick. One has a Red Sox tee shirt. If we go to where McDowell enters Scottsdale we can get eyes on them. Ed thinks they'll be by in less than ten minutes."

Bob got up from his seat. "Great. We're almost there now."

They parked at the northern entrance to Papago Park to watch the traffic eastbound on McDowell Road. Eleven minutes later they saw a white sedan coming east from Phoenix. As it approached the intersection, they observed two men in a Buick. A few seconds later Bob made a right turn and approached the car to read the rear license plate, and then stayed about twelve car lengths back.

Christy called in the plate number to dispatch. Two minutes later, she received a callback. The car was a rental from Sky Harbor airport, rented to a man from Chicago. They saw the Buick turn north at McClintock and they followed, staying just in observable range. Just north of Camelback Road they saw the Buick pull in and go behind the Blue Pony lounge.

A half-minute later Bob pulled into the parking lot and slowly drove to the back of the building. He parked where they could see the Buick, close to the rear door.

"I've heard of this place, but I've never been inside," said Christy. "It's kind of a low life hang out."

"Let's go in the front door as a casual couple and see what kind of place it is," said Bob.

The lounge stood by itself near a bowling alley and a family restaurant. It was a brick-faced concrete block building with no windows at the front. The entry way had a short vestibule to prevent the bright sunshine from flooding into the interior. The bar ran along the length of the building on the right on entering, and terminated at the back in what appeared to be a walk-in refrigerator. The expanse of the interior was set up with small round tables that would seat from two to four people. The lighting was soft and there was a TV operating over the bar. They saw an entrance to a room off the back end of the bar. To Bob, this place looked like a non-descript neighborhood bar. Several tables at the back were occupied with men in conversation. Bob and Christy sat down near the front. They were the only couple in the place. There were no overt stares, but Bob noticed covert glances from everyone. The bartender came to the end of the bar and asked, "What can I get you folks?"

Bob got up and went to the bar. "We'd like a couple of cold Coors Lite."

The bartender opened two bottles and placed them in front of Bob along with two glasses. "The tap isn't working right now." He turned and rang up the tab on the register.

Bob took the bottles and glasses back to the table. "Tap isn't working."

"So long as it's cold."

Christy filled her glass and turned to Bob. She spoke softly. "I think the guys in the Buick are seated at the far side, close to the bar."

"I see them. There's no way to be sure. It looks like the shorter guy put on a blue short sleeve shirt on top of his white t-shirt."

"I want to wait until one of them gets up to get a good look at them and see what's printed on his tee shirt."

"We might've already seen those two bastards…with full face masks," said Bob.

In a whisper Christy said, "I'm going to play with my phone camera. I'd really like to sneak a photo of those two."

"Be careful. Make sure the flash is off."

"Okay. I'll toy with it for a bit first. Get those boys used to it."

"Careful. We don't know who those guys are." He whispered, "I wonder if this is a mob hangout?"

"It has a rough reputation. Bar tender is staying at our end of the bar, probably straining to hear us."

Bob and Christy toyed with her phone and playfully took photos of each other. A minute later, the bartender lifted the gate at their end of the bar and came to their table. He scowled and pointed to a hand printed card at the bar.

"Sorry folks, we don't allow cameras to be used in here."

Bob shrugged. "Okay. Sorry."

Christy put the phone in her purse. When the bartender walked away, Christy whispered, "I hope I got a useful photo."

Bob smiled and nodded.

The front door to the lounge opened suddenly and three men came in. They walked along the bar and went directly into the back room. They each carried a pilot type map case.

Bob looked at Christy and whispered, "Drugs or money?"

She bumped his arm as the two men they had been interested in abruptly got up and also went into the back room. Although one man was noticeably shorter than the other, Bob couldn't say he recognized them from the altercation in the alley.

Christy whispered, "We should leave. I want to get the license numbers in the rear."

Bob placed some bills on the table as they got up to leave.

That evening, Bob and Christy went for a steak at Dante's in Tempe, an old establishment near the Mill Avenue Bridge. They sipped a cocktail before ordering their dinner. Christy brought up a nagging suspicion. "I've been thinking…Carmine's wife might have engineered the demise of the old boy."

"Sounds plausible, but I have to wonder just what the incentive was."

She grinned, "The usual things – sex, power and money."

Bob didn't immediately agree with Christy.

"What?"

"Just wondering how it would play out. Are you thinking Carmine's wife planned a coup with someone's help, but whom?"

"Maybe there's an arrangement between Carmine's wife and Frank to move him officially to the top of the family," she suggested.

Bob shook his head slowly. "Carmine already had Frank running things. I can't see what would be in it for her."

"I've been wondering whether the two men who murdered Carmine…and Laura…were specialists brought in just for the Carmine job or whether they're here to do other jobs."

"I've been wondering that myself," said Bob.

"If they were brought in just to do Carmine, don't you think they would have been on a plane back to wherever shortly thereafter?"

"Makes sense. I have to wonder though, how many operations are in play and who is pulling the strings?"

Their meals arrived with another round of drinks. The steaks were sizzling on the plates.

"Wow, this looks good," said Christy as she cut into it.

"I never had a bad meal here. I'll enjoy this."

All the tables in the large dining room were occupied mostly with couples. Bob saw that one table had older businessmen, seemingly each one trying to outdo the others with their point of view. One was on his cell phone. Bob turned back to Christy who had been glancing at him.

"You seem a little nervous," said Christy. "You okay?"

Bob nodded. "The trouble the other day at lunch has me a little on edge."

"Finish your meal and quit worrying." Christy grinned. "Besides, you're sitting with a cop."

"A damned pretty one at that."

"There you go. Now quit worrying."

As Bob finished his meal he stole glances at the group of men, not really sure why. The man with the cell phone got up, left the table, and disappeared into the kitchen.

"Are you still upset about the slow progress on Laura's murder?"

Bob grimaced. "Slow progress? No progress. I'm very disappointed at there being no suspect in her murder."

Christy sighed. "We haven't developed any useful clues and frankly, we are at a loss in what direction to pursue. There's been several people interviewed that had been in the area that day, but we didn't learn anything. We pulled in some fairly reliable snitches but didn't get anything from them."

"What about the images from the video cameras in the hotel where Carmine and Laura were murdered? Nothing new there?"

She shook her head. "It showed two men entered the hotel wearing identical realistic masks. The identity of the men could not be made. We did make an inquiry to the Phoenix FBI office hoping they might get something from the vague description of the two hit men. But I haven't heard back."

As they left Dante's that evening and walked into the rear parking area, Bob was alerted to the screaming sound of a dirt bike engine being started. He didn't see it but knew it was nearby. It seemed to be out of place at the up-scale restaurant. The whine of the motorcycle sound indicated it was approaching fast from nearby and he suddenly caught sight of it. He abruptly pushed Christy to be shielded beside a minivan, while he leapt to be behind a dumpster.

The burp of automatic gunfire and the resulting metallic rattle against the dumpster frightened Bob as he squatted amongst the debris on the ground. A cloud of noxious exhaust smoke surrounded him as the motorcycle sped off into the darkness. He stood up and looked toward Christy as he tried to quell his trembling.

"Bob!" She was suddenly in front of him hugging him and yelling into her cell phone. They held each other until the Tempe police arrived and took statements from them and others.

When the commotion quieted Christy and Bob got into his car, both were shocked and frightened by the attack.

"What the hell happened? I can't believe this," said Bob.

"Bob. Oh God, I sure hope that was mistaken identity."

"Shoot me? What kind of threat am I to anyone?"

They agreed there might be more to what happened with the Carmine shooting than they were aware of.

"I wonder if your letter to the editor got someone worried…worried enough to do this."

Bob shook his head. "Hard for me to believe…but still."

They nervously drove over the Salt River Bridge, passed the zoo, and turned onto the Galvin Parkway. They went through Papago Park intending to turn east into Scottsdale at McDowell Road. Suddenly, as they neared McDowell Road, a single bobbing headlight was seen approaching rapidly from the rear.

"Oh shit!" Bob held his gaze on the mirror.

Christy turned to look through the back window. "Bob! Is it the same guy? Oh Jesus!"

"Christy! Get down. Get down!"

Automatic gunfire slapped into the car. Windows shattered. Glass splattered the interior. Christy had her head down on the seat. Bob jammed on the brakes as the motorcycle sped by spewing gunfire into the car. The car came to an abrupt stop in loose gravel off the road. Christy pulled her pistol from her purse.

"Bob! Bob! Oh Christ, Bob." She saw Bob leaning against the shattered window, his face bloody.

He moaned loudly.

Christy opened her door and stepped out with gun and phone at the ready. She yelled for help to a 9-1-1 operator as her eyes scanned the dark desert for the reappearance of the shooter. Christy called to Bob and he responded with a loud moan, giving her hope. She went to his door and cautiously opened it. The seatbelt held him in place. She gasped at the wound on his neck and on the side of his head. They were bleeding steadily.

Christy called again to 9-1-1 for an EMT and then called Scottsdale Police to alert them to what had happened to her and Bob. She could see Bob was seriously hurt. She made simple compress from a towel in the car and applied it to Bob's neck wound. Christy was shaken and fearful and kept looking into the darkness for the return of the shooter. Scottsdale and Phoenix patrols arrived within minutes. Christy asked the EMTs to take Bob and her to Mountain View General Hospital in north Scottsdale. Phoenix PD took charge of the crime scene.

CHAPTER 16
BOB'S RECOVERY

Christy was told Bob was being treated in the ER for a skull fracture in the left temple and a fracture of the left shoulder blade, as well as a shallow neck wound. Meanwhile, Christy had glass particles removed from her face and hair. She again called her supervisor and reported her circumstances. Then she stayed in the waiting room, upset and frightened at what had happened to Bob. When she was told Bob had been admitted to the main hospital, she called Greg.

Greg arrived within thirty minutes and rushed to Christy's side. "What happened? Where's Bob? Is he okay?"

Christy put a hand on his shoulder. "Bob has just been admitted. We're told to stay in the waiting area until they tell us he can have visitors."

"What the hell happened? Tell me!"

"We were at Dante's, the parking lot in the back. Someone came at us on what sounded like a dirt bike and shot toward Bob with an automatic. I think the guy realized he had missed because he tried again when we were on Galvin Parkway. He shot up the car and wounded Bob."

Greg stared at her. "Were you hit?"

"No. They took out small pieces of glass from my face and in my hair."

"Why did this happen?" Greg was anxious and pacing around the room.

"Oh Greg, I wish I knew."

"Jesus, was it someone I pissed off?"

Christy shook her head. "I don't know."

A nurse walked up and told them it would be an hour or so before anyone could see Bob as he was still sedated. Christy called her office several times for updates on the investigation but was disappointed each time. Both of them paced and sat fidgeting in the waiting room for over an hour before the nurse permitted visitors to Bob's room.

"Just a few minutes," the nurse cautioned.

Greg went to Bob's bedside first, glad that Bob recognized him.

"Good to see you're awake. Can't believe what Christy told me."

"Glad you guys are here."

"Oh Bob, you gave us such a scare." Christy wiped at her eye with her hand. She bent over and kissed his lips.

"You're okay…didn't get hurt?"

"Just some glass pieces. Oh God, I was so worried about you. You were bleeding a lot. I couldn't tell where…"

"I'm sure happy to see you." He gave her a small grin. "I guess the evening didn't go so well."

She shook her head. "You sure know how to entertain a lady."

A nurse walked into the room and asked them to leave, as she wanted to give Bob medication for pain and to induce him to sleep. Greg said goodbye and that he would keep on top of the list of things they had agreed on. Christy caressed Bob's face and kissed him. Then she wiped away her tears with a brush of her hand.

Greg and Christy visited Bob separately the next day. They were allowed to stay longer. Greg assured Bob that he was checking on the list of fraudsters they had developed. Christy told him that Phoenix PD had been unable to identify the shooter. The bullets found in the car could not be matched to any of record. The FBI had not yet responded to her earlier inquiry.

Bob received a phone call on the second day. "Bob Wagner?"

"This is Bob."

"This is Frank. You doing okay?"

"I've had better days,"

"Listen to me. I think your attacker is going to want to finish the job. Stay away from your office and apartment for a while. These guys see you as some kind of witness to what happened with Carmine. You're a threat to them."

"What the hell…?"

"Just cool it. It'll work out." Then he hung up.

Bob stared at the ceiling in confusion. Frank calling me? Why? How could Frank be behind the murders and be calling and warning me? How could Christy be on the right track about Frank?

On the third day, the doctor said he wanted Bob to stay another day in the hospital, maybe longer, as there was still sign of infection and he was concerned with potential swelling of his brain. When Christy came to visit, Bob told her of the phone call.

Christy scowled. "You know what I think of Frank. He belongs in freakin' prison. But I have to insist that you pay attention to what he said."

"I'm rather surprised that he called."

"Yeah, well, he obviously knows things. I'm requesting PD keep a 24-hour patrol on this room as long as you're here."

"That'll get expensive."

"Don't sweat it. I'll make sure it happens."

"Thanks." Bob felt relieved.

"One more thing. I want you to stay at my apartment…for a while anyway. Greg can bring your clothes and take care of the clients."

"I really appreciate the offer, but I'll be okay at home. Greg can come by and bring me whatever."

"Don't give me that tough-guy stuff. You're staying at my place for a while." She smiled, "Get used to it."

Bob was hesitant to take advantage of Christy's offer, not wanting to be a burden on her, or bring danger to her at her apartment, as well as his own streak of independence. Christy insisted and said she didn't want to argue about it. He gave in.

The afternoon of the fifth day, Greg came to Bob's room with his clothes and toiletries. "Bob, you ready to get outa here? I got your stuff here."

Bob smiled as he swung his legs out of bed. "Bet your ass I'm ready. Have a seat while I do my thing in the bathroom."

The doctor had released him following satisfactory tests. The bandages on his head and on his shoulder hampered his movements. His neck and shoulder wounds gave him some pain for which he had been given prescription pain medicine. The head injury was the cause of intermittent headaches and distress. Greg helped Bob get dressed and with the orderly brought him out to the car. Christy had called Greg and told him to take Bob to her apartment, and when on the way to call and she'd meet them there.

- - - -

Christy arrived at her apartment a few minutes before Greg and Bob. The apartment was on the second level and Greg had to help Bob, still rather weak, to climb the stairs. Christy asked Greg to bring Bob into her bedroom and to remove Bob's clothes to leave only his boxer shorts.

"Wait a damn minute. I can do my own clothes."

Greg heard Bob grimace as he tried to get he pants down over his feet and went to him and pulled them off. "There, now get in bed."

"Damn it, I have to pee first."

After a trip to the toilet, Bob was tucked into bed and made comfortable with several pillows.

Greg handed Christy a hospital bag containing medications, prescriptions and Bob's personal items. He told Christy that he'd bring whatever she needed, just to call, as he had access to Bob's apartment and office. Soon after Bob took medicine for his pain, he fell fast asleep. Christy made a call to the police department and arranged for a round-the-clock patrol by her apartment.

Christy set her alarm to 11pm so she could give Bob his pain medicine and to check his temperature. She lay down with him until he was asleep, and then went back to her bed on the couch in the living room. The next morning, she made breakfast for both of them and helped Bob get to the kitchen table. She saw him grimace.

"Bob, your head hurting?"

"Yeah. I'll take a couple more ibuprofen. Sorry to be a burden."

She shook her head. "Shut up and eat your breakfast. Then we'll get you back to bed."

"I'd rather stay on the couch and watch TV. At least that gives me something to do."

When Bob was comfortable, she left for her job at the police station.

CHAPTER 17
UNDERSTANDINGS

The next day, Greg visited Bob at Christy's apartment as she arrived home from work. She made coffee and the three of them discussed possibilities for identifying the shooters of Bob, Carmine and Laura. They all wondered if there was one overall plan at work, or did these events have different origins?

"Who the hell is coming after Bob? That's what I want to know," demanded Greg. "We need to be ready if this happens again, don't we?"

"Yeah, Frank warned me," said Bob. "I think it's got to be someone in the Rinaldi gang."

"What someone?" asked Greg. "And why?"

"Lets go over things, see what we shake out," said Christy.

Christy summarized what she knew of the Carmine Palumbo murder. She had first heard of the murder from Gina Rossi who told of her conversation with Laura Jenkins.

Bob shifted his position on the couch, grimaced and then shook his head. "We've got to find those killers."

"We will," said Christy, "but it'll take a while. We don't have much to go on."

Greg asked, "You think this was a hit team from the Boston area?"

Christy shrugged. "I guess we all think so. But we can't assign blame yet. I still expect to receive a call from the Phoenix FBI that hopefully will shed some light on the two shooters. They have far better forensic equipment than we do in Scottsdale."

"I'm not going to hold my breath," groused Bob.

"Me neither," said Greg.

"Are there any new leads on the Jack Harvey hit?" asked Bob.

"We don't know much," said Christy. "It was confirmed, two bombs exploded under his car. The FBI are looking at the bomb pieces, see if they can figure out where the parts came from."

"Who is this Harvey guy, anyway?" asked Greg.

"He's a forty-year old Palumbo mob financier. It seems he was having an affair with an FBI agent living at the apartment building where Bob lives."

"No more pillow talk for him," said Bob.

Christy nodded.

"It's probably a safe assumption that Palumbo is responsible," said Bob.

"It maybe hard to prove until we get someone to talk," said Christy.

Greg spoke up. "Remember what I saw at Tony's Lounge with Mark Bianchi, Victor Diego and Rick Greene. That's got to be a Palumbo thing."

"Let's see," said Christy. "Bianchi was found dead in his Buick of a gunshot wound. He was a low-level soldier in the Palumbo organization with several arrests in Arizona but no convictions. As you know, they found him dead in his car at an intersection near his Phoenix home. In the trunk of his car was found the body of Victor Diego, a known Rinaldi associate." She looked at Bob. "Greg is sure Diego was killed by Palumbo associate Bianchi or a Palumbo soldier named Rick Greene to maybe cover up Greene's hit on Diego at Tony's Lounge in Phoenix."

"A lot to wrap one's head around," said Bob.

"Yep, now we have the Walter Schneider killing to consider," said Christy. "He was a very well known irritant to the Palumbo family. He also wrote about the Rinaldi guys every now and then. Just like the Harvey hit, it was two bombs under the car."

"No real suspects yet?" asked Greg.

"No. We have all the usual suspects being interviewed. I'm hopeful someone will talk."

"Is this the responsibility of one group or just one person?"

Christy shook her head. "The Boston guys are very likely shooters and not bombers. I think there's something else at play here."

"I didn't think I had serious enemies," said Bob. "Still, I can't put the blame on the Palumbo people…based on what Frank said to me."

Christy shook her head. "I can't agree with you on that. Your semi-friendly relationship with Frank might be troublesome to someone, even someone in the Palumbo outfit."

Bob nodded. "Gotta think about that."

"Please do. Someone's bound to try a hit on you again."

"What about Rick Greene?" asked Greg. "I'm almost certain he was involved in the murders of Victor Diego and Mark Bianchi. He is a Palumbo soldier."

"What are you thinking?" asked Christy.

"It's occurred to me that Greene could be a bomber *and* shooter and an all around fixer in the Palumbo organization."

"And what, he whacked Carmine and Laura?"

"Maybe had someone do it," said Greg.

"And you think he is responsible for the assault on Bob?"

"Don't know. But to me it's possible."

Christy shook her head. "Of course, it is possible. However, what does Frank Palumbo have to gain with the murder of Carmine? Frank is already acting head of the outfit by Carmine's directive."

"If the hit on Carmine was not sanctioned by Frank," said Bob, "that leaves only the Rinaldi outfit."

Greg nodded.

Christy grimaced and looked at Greg. "And the two bombings, you're thinking Greene for this?"

"It makes sense to me. But it's all guess work."

Christy brought out snacks and more coffee as they continued to talk about what the encroachment of Rinaldi operatives from Tucson into the Phoenix area would mean. This Chicago-based outfit had been well entrenched in Tucson businesses for many years. It seemed the dominance of the Palumbo outfit in Phoenix-Scottsdale area was being challenged. They all agreed that Rinaldi was likely moving drugs into Phoenix, as the Palumbo outfit was very weak in this market from the years-long disfavor by Carmine.

"Well, besides the question of who wants me dead, the standing question for me is who ordered the murder of Carmine?" said Bob. "And then, who actually did the murder of him and Laura?"

"Are we to think now, it was Rinaldi who ordered the hit?" asked Christy.

Bob and Greg nodded. "It makes a certain amount of sense," said Bob.

"And who pulled the trigger?"

"It's a bit of a stretch but if you put Greene secretly in the Rinaldi camp," said Bob, "then he could have arranged the hit."

Christy frowned. "This Greene guy hired the two east coast thugs to do the job? Wow. I don't know. There's nothing to support this idea."

Bob nodded. "But it's what I'm thinking."

"Makes sense to me," said Greg.

Christy shook her head. "Phoenix FBI owes me a return call with what information they can come up with on the two masked hit men. I'll query them again."

They discussed the dissension and division rumored in the Palumbo organization. What were the core values within the Palumbo organization that were being questioned and who was the source of dissension? Was the lack of an active drug business the issue driving dissension? What did the traitors expect to gain by a change in Palumbo leadership? Christy then asked whether the change in leadership was maybe personality driven.

"You mean that lack of drug sales isn't the driver to a change in leadership?" asked Greg.

Christy nodded. "Sure, the disallowance of a drug initiative is probably what's causing the dissatisfaction and restiveness. However, leadership has changed and now Frank is running things and likely to keep running things. I think Frank will loosen up the reins regarding drug sales. To me, the murder of Carmine at this time has to have another reason."

"I have to agree with that," said Bob glancing at Greg. "Christy makes a lot of sense."

"You were headed in that direction weren't you?"

"I wasn't saying it out loud, but yes."

Christy reminded the group Angelo Palumbo, nephew of Carmine and brother of Frank, was killed suspiciously two years ago at age 32 in what looked like a staged auto accident in Los Angeles.

"This was rumored to be a hit by the **Rinaldi** family," said Christy "But I don't really know. It never made much sense to me."

"Why, I wonder?" asked Greg. "To position Frank for the top job after Carmine?"

"It's plausible, but that's not clear to me either," said Christy.

"There's still Carmine's wife to contend with," said Bob shifting again in his chair.

Christy smiled. "Carmine was 76 years old. His second wife, Maria, is a far younger woman of 55 years. It might be prudent to question her loyalties."

"Are you serious?" asked Greg.

"Christy shrugged. "Just sayin'. I don't have any proof."

"If there's a personal relationship between Maria Palumbo and a Rinaldi guy," said Greg, "this could also be a source of dissention in the Palumbo family."

"I should think so."

"I'm thinking," said Bob, "if there is a relationship, it would suggest Maria Palumbo is the key person along with a Rinaldi dude as the sponsor of the hit on Carmine and therefore Laura."

"We're going to have to find out about this, somehow," said Greg.

Bob looked at Greg and nodded. "It could change everything."

"Staying within the law will be important," said Christy, "especially if you might want to use any of it in court."

Bob said, "I'm convinced the actual shooters were the two men we think are from the east, likely from Boston."

Christy said, "I'll press the Phoenix FBI to make identifications from the pictures obtained from area video cameras. I don't know why the FBI is slow walking my request; they might have their own interests here."

Bob scratched his chin. "What's the benefit to Maria Palumbo of a relationship with a Rinaldi guy? Is it the Rinaldi desire to influence the Palumbo outfit or is it a physical relationship, or maybe both?"

"Sounds like something you and Greg need to find out," said Christy smiling.

Greg asked Christy if she thought there was any benefit to the Rinaldi outfit from the Carmine murder.

Christy replied, "Yes, a hopeful foothold to expansion of their drug business. And the manipulation and eventual integration of the Palumbo outfit into the Rinaldi organization as the Palumbo outfit is further fragmented and may soon cease to exist in a practical sense. Just my opinion of course."

CHAPTER 18
NEXT STEPS

Christy had interviewed and cajoled many of her long-standing sources but had been unable to get actionable information on the killings of Bianchi and Victor Diego. Greg had pointed to Rick Greene as the likely killer of Bianchi, as Greene had been at the lounge when Diego was likely put in the trunk of the Buick. Christy was almost certain Mark Bianchi had been killed for being a traitor in the Palumbo family as well as to silence him regarding the killing of Diego. Also, he was probably killed as revenge for the earlier murder in LA of the brother of Frank Palumbo. She was frustrated and anxious to bring justice to this situation, but the DA wanted proof before any warrants would be issued.

She was certain Walter Schneider had been killed to stop the frequent assaults in the Valley Gazette against the Palumbo organization; although she admitted, Schneider hadn't left out Rinaldi in his criticisms. Every week for months there appeared Op-Ed pieces going into every aspect of the Palumbo family and their alleged criminal enterprises. She wondered if Greene indeed was the bomber in the Palumbo outfit as she and Bob had discussed. Although Greene seemed to be the go-to-guy to carry out deadly tasks in the Palumbo outfit, Christy hadn't read of explosives work in Greene's history. This was a high profile case she knew would bring demands for justice.

Christy decided to investigate whether, within the Scottsdale and Phoenix police departments, solid evidence existed in regard to recent drug sales by Rinaldi and Palumbo operatives. If so, squeezing these suspects might reveal names of Palumbo collaborators with Rinaldi, and could possibly be cultivated to become sources of information. Yesterday, she had heard that two Rinaldi thugs, who had been arrested for selling drugs, were currently in the Phoenix downtown jail waiting to be processed.

As an investigator with the Scottsdale Police, she had little leverage with investigations of Palumbo activities in Phoenix. However, Christy had become friendly with an older Phoenix police officer while attending a seminar in Las Vegas. So now, she picked up the phone and looked at one of many yellow sticky notes on the edge of her computer monitor and then punched in the number.

"Hello. May I speak to Officer Anderson?"

"Stuart Anderson speaking."

"This is Christy Holland, Scottsdale. Remember me?"

"Hello Christy. Sure I remember you. How've you been?"

"I stay busy. You're getting close to retirement, aren't you?"

"Well, yeah, a couple more years. What's up?"

"I understand Phoenix is investigating Rinaldi and Palumbo activity in the city. I think some of it is spreading to Scottsdale."

"Yeah, we run into those guys from time to time. Mesa and Tempe have had some problems, also. We're talking drugs, of course."

"What do you know of the Rinaldi guys moving in from Tucson?"

"We've got a couple of their low-life's sitting in the pokey right now. They were brought in yesterday, one for selling stuff to an undercover officer, and the other with a kilo in his car. They weren't in our system, but they'll be in front of a judge by tonight."

"Do you think I could get a crack at them?"

"What do you hope to gain? I think these guys are just gofers."

"I'd like to find out what the Rinaldi outfit is thinking regarding spreading out, particularly into Scottsdale."

"Well, you're certainly welcome to interview them. But, we can't offer them any consideration."

"I understand and appreciate the opportunity. I'll call before I come over."

"Good. It'll be nice to see you again."

Christy's phone rang when she hung up with Stuart Anderson.

"Officer Holland."

"This is Ron Oscar in Image Identification."

"Working on the two suspects for me?"

"We've done all we can with the images. They are still not clear enough with our equipment to recognize them and come up with names. The feds been any help?"

"I thought I would have heard from them by now. But not yet."

"We can't do anything more on this; maybe if we get new software."

"Okay. Thanks a lot for trying."

"Sure"

Christy disconnected.

- - - -

Greg had planned to drive by the gated entrance to the Carmine Palumbo home every few days while Bob recovered from his wounds. Hoping to discover Maria's paramour, he found a parking place on a nearby rise, close by another large and pricey home. The parking spot allowed a good view of the front of the Palumbo home as well as their driveway and parking area. Using high-power binoculars, he took note of the comings and goings through the large gate. Although he logged several cars going in and out of the estate, it became obvious after a few days there were only a few different visitors.

Late in the third afternoon, a Scottsdale Police cruiser pulled up behind Greg. The officer got out of his car and approached Greg who lowered his window.

"What are you doing here, sir?"

"I work for Confidential Investigations." Greg handed his driver's license to the officer. Then he handed him a business card with his name on it as well as that of Bob Wagner.

"Like I said…Mr. Auburn…what are you doing here?"

"I'm supposed to see who comes and goes over at the Palumbo place."

The officer stared at Greg. "Why are you doing this?"

"It's my job." Greg tried to seem casual and bored.

"You think the Palumbo household is going to appreciate finding out you're spying on them?"

Greg shrugged. "Maybe not."

The officer wrote something in his notebook before handing the ID back to Greg. "Get out of here. I see you back here again, we'll have a conversation about this back at the station." He got back into his cruiser and drove away.

Greg started the engine. He assumed the officer would be on the phone to the Palumbo place in short order.

- - - -

Christy had just hung up on a call from Greg who informed her that he had been warned by a Scottsdale officer to abandon his spying of the Palumbo estate. She asked him to be discrete and said she couldn't offer him any cover if he was caught. Then she placed a call to Stuart Anderson of the Phoenix PD. The call was answered on the fourth ring.

"Anderson."

"Stuart, this Christy Holland. You have a minute?"

"Uh, sure. What's up?"

"Do you still have the two characters you mentioned available? I'd like to interview them."

"We can still do that. Lawyers were just with them."

"Probably a waste of both of our time; but what the hell, I'll give it a try."

"Remember, we can't give them any consideration. They either talk to you or they don't. I'll be sitting in with you."

"Sure. That'll be fine. I won't take up a lot of your time."

"Okay. An hour from now?"

"Thanks. I'll see you then."

Christy found a parking spot on Adams Street and walked into the Phoenix PD. She asked for Officer Anderson at the lobby. He came and signed her in. As they walked to the Interview Rooms, Anderson again cautioned her. "Remember, you can't suggest any cooperation or consideration. All meetings are recorded."

Christy nodded and smiled. "I understand. I don't expect much from these guys, but I have to try."

"Yeah, why not."

Near the end of the corridor, Anderson stopped. "Here we are. I have them in Interview 3 and 4." He looked at his note pad. "We'll do Paul Salerno first. He's in 4."

A guard standing by room 4 opened the door and stepped inside followed by Anderson and Christy. The guard left the room, the door closed, and Anderson gestured to a chair for Christy to sit facing the prisoner. Anderson stood against the wall between the door and Salerno.

Anderson spoke, "Mr. Salerno, this is Officer Holland of Scottsdale PD. She'd like a few words with you."

Salerno looked blankly at Christy. "How 'bout we get rid of these things?" Salerno shook the handcuffs.

"You wish," said Anderson.

"Mr. Salerno, I understand you're up here from Tucson." Christy smiled. "What brings you up this way? Selling shit?"

He scowled and shrugged. "Tryin' to make a buck."

"How old are you?"

"Screw off."

Anderson took a step toward Salerno and swatted him upside the head. "Speak up. We can't hear you."

"Hey! You got no fuckin' call."

Anderson slapped him again. "Watch your mouth."

Christy asked, "You have folks or friends up this way?"

"No."

"So…you go back to Tucson on the weekend?"

Again a shrug. "Sometimes. Just tryin' to make a buck." He slouched down lower in his chair.

"You bring the stuff up here from Tucson, and then what? Where do you deliver it?"

"I don't know nothin' about that."

"Sure you do. You tried to sell some shit to an officer. Bad luck, huh?"

Salerno scowled and stared at the tabletop.

"Rinaldi guys will be ticked off…you not making any money and you lost the junk."

"Who?"

"The guys you're working for. What else you do for them?"

"Nothing."

"Where do you deliver the stuff you bring up here?"

Salerno shook his head. "Stuff?"

"You bring shit up from Tucson. Where do you take it?"

He looked down at the tabletop. "Forget it. You can't do anything for me."

"She can't, wise guy," said Anderson, "but maybe I can. So talk to her."

Salerno glanced at Anderson and scowled. "I want outa here."

"You haven't given us squat, so sit tight. You'll be in front of a judge in less than an hour."

"The Glass Slipper," he mumbled.

"Huh? What's that?" said Anderson.

Salerno looked at Anderson. "On 35th Avenue. He owns the place."

"Rinaldi owns the Glass Slipper?"

"What'd I just say? Am I gonna get out of here?"

"That's all you got?"

Salerno looked at Christy. "Silk and Satin."

"Downtown Scottsdale?" said Christy. "You yanking my chain?"

"He now owns the place…or at least most of it."

"And what, you deliver stuff to these places?"

Salerno shook his cuffs. "Am I outa here or what?"

Christy looked at Anderson and then at Salerno. "How do you know this?"

He shrugged. "Buggsy… he lets me flop in the back room at the Slipper. I hang out there until I gotta do an errand or something."

"Who's he? The bartender?"

"Yeah."

"You drive for Rinaldi?"

"Sometimes."

"You ever drive up to the Palumbo place? Pick up Maria Palumbo?"

"Yeah. So, am I outa here or what?"

Anderson stepped closer to the door. "We'll talk about it. Sit tight." He turned to Christy and nodded toward the door.

In the hallway, he asked Christy, "You got enough?"

"Yes. Thanks for your help. Appreciate it." She gave him her best smile. "You think I could get a copy of the audio?"

Anderson sighed. "Uh-huh. You still need to talk to the other dude?"

"What do you know about him?"

He shrugged. "They came up from Tucson together. I didn't know about the Rinaldi thing. Hadn't thought to ask."

"I think I have enough. This has been helpful. I appreciate it." She turned to look at him. "Can we get the tape?"

"Don't see why not. Let me check with the captain."

They started toward the stairs.

- - - -

The next day Greg was determined to get a photo of Maria and her male friend. He had seen a silver Mercedes enter and then leave the Carmine Palumbo estate the previous day. Today, he wanted to be certain Maria Palumbo was the passenger. He eased up on the accelerator. The digital camera was ready on the seat beside him, and he was hopeful of a quick photo of the woman and her escort.

He stayed several cars behind the Mercedes as they traveled toward north Phoenix. Just before Central Avenue, the Mercedes turned north and soon pulled into an old but luxurious apartment complex. Greg slowed, allowing the Mercedes to fully enter the parking lot before following. He hung back and grabbed his camera. He readied it for rapid-sequence shots and slowly approached the now parked car. His first few pictures captured the driver getting out of the car. Greg moved ahead a few yards and shot a series of pictures as the man opened the passenger door and helped the woman out of the car. He drove slowly ahead, confident his darkened windows had shielded him even though he didn't think the two people had been paying attention.

Greg was pleased with himself, hoping he had proof of his suspicions. He would study the pictures carefully on his computer, but felt fairly sure he had captured Maria with her paramour. He pulled into the parking area of Confidential Investigations and entered the building. The air-conditioned coolness pleased him after hours in his hot car. The mailbox was crammed with junk mail and bills. He scooped it all up and took it up to the office. Greg fumbled in his pocket for the key to the office door and finally it swung open. He dumped the mail on the conference table and then went to the computer on Bob's desk. When the computer came alive, Greg glanced to the left side of the keyboard, smiled and typed in 1qaz as the password.

He booted up the photo editor and plugged in the memory card from the camera. The photos were not perfect, having some blurriness, but were adequate to see facial features of the male driver and Maria Palumbo. Greg then opened the file that Bob had made that showed facial images of hundreds of people he had come in contact with, most surreptitiously obtained. He quickly verified the photo of Maria Palumbo, but the male face was not someone he was sure of. He hoped that Bob or Christy would be able to identify the person. He sent an email to Christy and asked if she could identify the male with Maria.

- - - -

First thing the next morning, Christy opened the e-mail from Greg and read his query. She studied the face of the driver in the car with Maria and was surprised to recognize the male as the dude she had recently interviewed. It certainly wasn't Maria's lover, but Paul Salerno working as a driver.

Damn, the guy got released on bail. She had interviewed the Rinaldi gopher in Phoenix the day before. Christy called Greg and they agreed Maria's lover probably lived in one of the apartments, but remained unidentified.

Greg had seen the driver stop in front of apartment building number four. The two-story building contained 24 units. Greg hoped he wouldn't get challenged as he walked into the foyer entryway later that afternoon. There he took photos of the mailboxes. The boxes all had labels identifying the apartment number, but not the name, unfortunately.

Greg, not to be dissuaded, called the phone number on the trash dumpster and asked when the pickup was scheduled. He was told that under normal circumstances, trash pickup would occur around 8am Thursday morning. The next day was Wednesday, so Greg donned some old clothes and at 9pm he entered the side door of the big dumpster with a flashlight. His objective was to identify the unit numbers and the associated name of male occupants by searching discarded items of mail. After an hour, he was successful in obtaining twenty names and apartment numbers, mainly from discarded utility bills. Some apartments had not discharged trash that day. Afterward, he went home, tossed his clothes in the laundry hamper and took a hot shower.

The next day Greg visited Bob, still recuperating at Christy's apartment. Bob was by himself and resting on the couch in front of the TV. Greg assured him that he had maintained his monitoring of the suspects requested by Workers Comp. Then he described his efforts to find out whom Maria Palumbo was seeing on the sly.

Bob chuckled. "You spent an hour dumpster diving? You kidding me?"

"Yep," Greg scowled. "I'll give you my laundry bill."

Bob shook his head. "What did you find? Anything useful? You're not bringing me a disease are you?"

"I'm not itching yet," Greg chuckled. "I got twenty names of men in that building and their apartment numbers. I may have missed one or two."

"Let's take a look at the list. I'll see if any names jump out at me."

Greg pulled the list of names from his back pocket and unfolded it, smoothing out the folds as he laid it on the coffee table. Bob read through the list and asked Greg for a pen. He made a check mark next to Tony Romano.

He handed the paper to Greg. "I recall this guy. He's a made-man with Rinaldi and has been for a long time. He's never been indicted, at least not here in Arizona. I can certainly believe that he and Maria could an item. Why don't you text the name to Christy and ask what she thinks?"

Greg nodded, picked up the paper, and opened his cell phone. After he sent the message to Christy's phone, he went into Bob's kitchen.

"You want more coffee, Bob?"

"I'm good. Help yourself."

They didn't have long to wait. Ten minutes later, Bob's cell phone rang. He muted the TV and answered the call. "Hi, Christy. You saw what Greg sent you?"

"I just did. I'm not going to ask how you came up with this name. It's an interesting choice. I'll try to confirm it."

"Anything you can tell me?"

"I can tell you that he has a sheet from Chicago but has never been indicted in Arizona. He's close to Rinaldi and manages to keep his hands clean."

"I'm almost certain he and Maria are a pair and they may be up to something," said Bob.

"I wonder if your friend Frank would agree with that."

"I don't dare ask him."

She chuckled, "Best if you didn't."

"Thanks, Christy. Talk to you later." Bob disconnected the call and turned to Greg. "She won't say what, but I'm sure she thinks those two are up to something."

Greg nodded. "Maybe we'll soon know if Carmine's wife was a traitor as well as being an adulterer."

"Listen Greg, it's important to take care of all the requests we get from insurance companies and Workman's Comp. You think you can do all this by yourself?"

"I'll manage. I will need a check from you soon. It's been a rough couple weeks."

"You're right. I'm sorry. Please bring me the company checkbook out of my desk."

"Okay. It's getting late in the day. I'll stop by the office now and see what's in the mail and check e-mail. I'll come by tomorrow."

"Thanks, Greg."

Greg parked his aging car under the shaded area behind the office building where Bob usually parked. He got out of the car, pocketed his keys and headed toward the back entrance of the building. Just before reaching the door, two men stepped out from behind a car. He didn't recognize them. A chill went up his back as one man stepped to be behind him as the other blocked his way to the entrance.

"Hey! Greg is it? We've been waiting for you to show up. What took you so long? It's freakin' hot out here."

Greg didn't see a way to escape. "What do you guys want? Who the hell are you?"

Suddenly the man behind Greg grabbed his arms and clamped them helplessly to his side. The man in front slammed a fist into Greg's midsection. He recoiled in pain and gasped for breath.

"Greg baby! Do I have your attention now?"

Greg gasped for breath and moaned.

"What? Speak up."

"What…the hell…you want?"

"Greg baby! I'm told you've been snooping around where you have no business being. Now, we're here to tell you, real friendly like, that you can't keep on doing this because it really won't be good for your health." The man reached over and patted Greg on the cheek. "Are we getting through to you or what?"

Greg nodded.

"What's that? Speak up."

"Yeah. I got it."

"We think you need to convince your boss that it's not a good idea to go poking around other peoples business and stirring up shit. Think you can do that?"

Greg nodded. "Uh-huh."

The man slammed his fist into Greg again.

Greg gasped and spit out bile and recoiled in pain. "You miserable bastards," he gasped.

"You guys spying around, leaving footprints on web sites you shouldn't be on, and arousing suspicion with the po-lice. We're not going to tell you again, this has to stop. You make sure your boss understands. You hear?"

"Fuck off."

"What?" The man in front of Greg swung a backhand across Greg's face. "Greg baby, this was just a friendly suggestion. You don't want us to have to come back and remind you. So wise up." The man firmly patted Greg on the cheek.

The man pinning Greg's arms let him loose and pushed him away. The two men then disappeared quickly behind some cars. Greg fell to the ground and then stumbled toward the building. He accessed the key-code controlled door, and stood inside welcoming cool air on his face. He took refuge in the nearby men's room to wash his face and straighten his appearance; then sat on a bench to gather his thoughts and calm his nerves.

He usually took the stairs to the second floor office, but he gave in to his discomfort and pushed the button for the elevator. On reaching Confidential Investigations, he unlocked the door to the outer area and then unlocked the door to Bob's office. Feeling nauseous, he lay down on the couch and within minutes he was asleep.

- - - - -

Greg had been gone less than an hour when Bob decided to call him to ask what mail there was from customers. He wasn't able to get Greg to answer the office phone. He then called his cell phone, but that went unanswered as well. A sense of alarm gripped Bob. After trying again to reach Greg, he placed a call to Christy.

"Hello Bob. I'm just wrapping up here. You need something?"

"I've been trying to get a hold of Greg…calling the office and his cell phone. He was here an hour ago, but now I can't reach him. I'm worried. He's been doing some snooping around and he…"

"Slow down, Bob. I'm done here in about fifteen minutes. I'll go by your office and see if he's there. I'll be in touch."

"Thanks, Christy." The call disconnected.

- - - - -

Christy parked her car next to Greg's old Nissan. She looked through the car windows but nothing there alarmed her. Her special key card was able to open the rear door and she soon entered Confidential Investigations. She found Greg face down on the couch. Alarmed, she checked for a pulse and felt he was warm. Relieved that he was asleep, but concerned at seeing a number of soiled tissues next to him on the floor, she shook him to awaken him.

"Greg. Greg. Wake up. Talk to me."

He opened his eyes. "Huh? Christy?"

"Yes. Are you ill? What's wrong? Jesus, your face, what the hell happened?"

"I got waylaid when I parked my car. A pair of goons worked me over."

"Are you hurt? Sick? Talk to me."

"I'll be okay. Lost my lunch." He looked down at the pile of soiled tissues.

"You want a doctor? I can drive you to the ER."

"Thanks. No." He looked at her. "How come you're here?"

"Bob was trying to call you. Said he couldn't reach you. He was worried. I said I'd come by and see if you were okay."

"Thanks."

"Why did this happen? What did they want?"

"It was a warning…to keep out of their business. I've been snooping around."

"Who did this? Do you know?"

Greg shook his head. "Never seen them before. Two guys."

"Do you have working cameras around the building?"

"I saw one out back near the door. Don't know if it works."

"Okay. You call Bob and tell him what's going on. I'm going to check out the camera. I'll call the building manager."

Christy left the office and went down to the back door. Outside, she saw a camera just to one side of the doorway and about fifteen feet off the ground. The phone number for the building manager was stenciled on the glass panel next to the door. She called and the manager agreed to come to the building right away to allow Christy to review the images on the recorder. The recording equipment was in a small closet near the front of the building. On the monitor, she saw that one man was significantly taller than the other; prompting her to wonder if the two men were the culprits they've been after for the Carmine and Laura murders. She sent a copy of the images to the forensics desk at Scottsdale Police and asked them to enhance the faces for identification.

CHAPTER 19

BOLO

Bob answered his phone on the fourth ring and was pleased to hear Christy's voice.

"Bob, did you hear from Greg?"

"Yes. He called and told me what happened. He said you were looking at what the video camera might show."

"I had the manager come over and I got a copy of the video. I sent it to the computer forensics desk at Scottsdale PD. The images showed two white men roughing up Greg."

"Any chance to identify them?"

"PD had records on them as two known hoodlums in the Rinaldi organization."

"Can you pick them up?" asked Bob.

"I requested arrest warrants from the DA."

"How is Greg doing?"

"He's pretty bruised up. He'll be okay, nothing broken."

"Thanks for looking in on him," said Bob.

"We need to talk about what those goons wanted. This won't stop, I'm afraid."

"Yeah, I'm sorry Greg got hurt. You sure he's okay?"

"He's hurting, but he'll be okay. You're obviously getting close to the wrong people. They hurt Greg this time because they couldn't get to you."

"Makes me very angry."

"We have to talk about this."

Although sore from the bruises, Greg helped Bob return to his own apartment the next morning. He made sure Bob was comfortable and well situated before resuming the task of checking on suspicious clients of the Worker's Comp Program. Bob asked him not to go by Maria or Tony's residence for the time being as he didn't want him to get hurt again.

That afternoon Bob felt well enough to drive himself to his office. He stopped at Dunkin' Donuts to pick up a muffin and a large coffee. He sat at his desk, appreciating the comfort of his well-worn leather-upholstered chair and the familiar taste of the DD coffee. The phone rang a few minutes before four.

"Confidential Investigations, Bob Wagner speaking."

"This is Frank. I'm glad to hear you recovered."

"Thanks. I can get around, but I'm not altogether well."

"Say, you got this guy working for you…what's his name? Greg?"

"Yeah. He's helping me."

"Uh-huh. I hear he's getting some folks pissed off."

"Oh for crissakes, he was assaulted the other day; beat up right outside the office here."

"I hear people are getting pissed off."

"It ain't right. He's just a young guy doing stuff for me since I've been laid up."

"None of my guys."

"You sure?"

"You want I should repeat myself?" His voice took a sterner tone.

There was an uncomfortable pause.

"Who are you thinking? People I'm looking at?"

"As you can imagine, I have my own problems these days. We might have something in common, though."

"Maybe…"

"You think about that. Take care, now." The phone went dead.

Bob muttered, "Something in common? Like what?"

Was Frank steering him to the Rinaldi outfit? Were the two outfits coming in conflict here, in the Phoenix area? Did the killing of Carmine Palumbo have multiple threads? He'd had a hunch that Carmine's wife, Maria, had been involved in some way and that it wasn't just about having a stud pony on the side. He wondered, who exactly is Maria? Where did she come from to capture Carmine's eye? Having a lover in the Rinaldi outfit, if indeed it was true, might mean a takeover of the Palumbo outfit was planned. A bloodless coup might be what Rinaldi and Maria were planning. Bob shook his head, all this was just conjecture. More work had to be done. Had elimination of Carmine been the first step?

Bob picked up his cell phone and pressed a button to call Greg. He worried about his safety.

"Hey, what's up?"

"Where are you?"

"Sitting near ASU waiting for a dead-beat-dad to make a move. He's like six months in arrears. If he's working, I need to find out where and call it in."

"Okay. I'm still in some pain and trying to stay in the office. The thing that's been bothering me is: who is Maria exactly? I need to find out where she came from and how she managed to latch onto Carmine. I think we can be sure it wasn't for sex."

Greg chuckled. "That's probably a sure bet. Everything that's happened around here may well have a string to her. What do you want me to do?"

"I'm just thinking out loud, but we may have to tug on some of those strings to shake something loose. I'll work on it from here."

"Okay. I'll be in touch." Greg disconnected.

Bob put the phone down, but then picked it up again and pushed the button for Christy. Her phone rang twice.

"Hey you."

"Just a curious question," said Bob.

"Does it have to do with sex?"

"I could probably work that in later."

"I don't think so. You pull a stitch and you'll be back in the hospital."

"Well, okay…for now," said Bob. "Anyhow, I'm wondering where to look or who to ask to figure out where Maria Palumbo came from. How did she meet and latch onto Carmine? How did she meet Carlos Rinaldi?"

"She came down from Chicago a couple years back, as I recall."

"Then what? She latched onto Carlos?" said Bob. "And then she got together with Tony Romano on the sly? Wow, she's been busy."

"Frankly, I'm not sure of the history. I know that Romano spent most of his years in Chicago. He came down to this area in the last couple."

"He met Maria down here?"

"I guess so," said Christy. "For sure, her various drivers are people assigned by Romano. That'd keep the relationship from getting too much publicity."

"Anything new on the two creeps that hit on Greg?"

"No. We're looking for them."

"They're not the guys that hit Carmine and Laura?"

"No, these are a couple of Rinaldi thugs. The two guys we assume from back East know they're hot and that we're looking for them," said Christy. "If they're still here, it means Rinaldi is keeping them on ice."

"You haven't heard anything at all?"

"Not yet."

"I told Greg to back off from Romano and Maria for the time being. I hate putting him in anymore danger."

"He's a loyal guy. You should treat him right."

"I can't give him much of a salary," said Bob. "However, when I get a check from one of the agencies, I give him a bonus. He seems happy with that."

"He's a hard worker."

"I keep him busy checking on the dead beats and fraudsters," said Bob. "It's a never-ending routine. But he also keeps an eye on certain suspects for me."

"I don't think I want to know too much."

"By the way, I received a brief call from Frank Palumbo."

"What? When? What the heck he want?"

"About an hour ago. Reason he called was to deny that any of his guys did anything to Greg."

"You believe him?"

"When I questioned him, he started to get angry. I think he believes none of his guys had anything to do with it. He might be right. The two guys that slapped Greg around might well be Rinaldi goons delivering some sort of message about spying on Maria and Tony."

"You've got some strange friends, Bob."

"Maybe. I was useful to Frank a couple years back and now he thinks he's being a good guy."

"A shaky relationship…"

"Can you give me a heads-up when you hear anything about the two thugs?"

"Sure."

"Thanks. Miss you."

"Me too. G'bye."

CHAPTER 20

INQUIRIES

Bob looked at his watch. It was 3:30, still time to make a call to the Valley Gazette. He had called Dennis Schilling of the Organized Crime Desk a year ago to inquire as to their understanding of possible mob involvement in Workers Comp fraud. But now, Bob wanted to hear what they had to say regarding their investigations of Palumbo and Rinaldi criminal activity.

Bob started the conversation with Schilling by offering his condolences over the murder of their reporter. "Hi Dennis, I'm sorry about what happened to Walter Schneider. He and I had occasional conversations on the goings-on in the state."

"Yes, it was a dastardly thing to have happened. It's a great loss here and for his family."

"I always thought of him as a fine reporter. He did excellent work in the investigation of the Palumbo and Rinaldi relationship following the murder of Carmine."

As the two men conversed, Schilling stated as fact that Maria (Sanatoria) had met Carlos Rinaldi in one of his Chicago clubs, where she had worked as a cocktail waitress.

"Carlos took a liking to her," said Dennis. "He put her up in fine style."

"But then she came here?"

"Yes. A few years ago she moved to Scottsdale and got close to Carmine Palumbo. It wasn't long before she was married to him."

"Was she two-timing it with the Rinaldi people?"

"Well, it wasn't long afterward Maria met and became secretly cozy with Tony Romano, a made-man in the Rinaldi outfit."

"Wow. Interesting."

"Yep. Schneider had photographic evidence of the pair in several meetings. A short time later, two men murdered Carmine Palumbo."

"Do you have a lead on the two killers?"

"I don't want to say who I think the two killers might be, as I don't have any real evidence."

Schilling told Bob he favored Rinaldi as the instigator of the event as he had the most to gain.

When Bob asked about Rinaldi people moving into the Phoenix-Scottsdale area from Tucson, Schilling enthusiastically said that Rinaldi had been investing in the area for a couple of years. He was sure they would become the dominant mob group in another year or two.

- - - - -

Christy visited Bob at his office in late afternoon. He told her about his conversation with Schilling. A few minutes later, Greg arrived from a stakeout of a suspect claiming Workers Comp following an employment accident.

"Anything new?" Greg looked at Christy.

She shook her head. "Those responsible for the assault on you have been identified and we're looking for them. No surprise, they are associated with Rinaldi. What about you? What's going on?"

"I've been watching and photographing the movements of Rick Greene as a Workers Comp fraudster."

"You're still thinking Greene is responsible for the hit on Diego and Bianchi?"

"As I told you some time ago, when I was staked out at Tony's Lounge I saw Greene help put a rolled up rug into the trunk of a Buick with Mark Bianchi. After the car drove off, I'm fairly sure Rick Greene walked through the lounge and out a door on the opposite side of the building."

"Too bad we don't have solid proof."

"I can't prove it, but I believe Greene got into a parked car and followed and killed Mark Bianchi who later was found dead of a gunshot in his Buick at an intersection near his Phoenix home. In the trunk of the car, the Phoenix police found the body of Victor Diego. I believe Greene killed Victor Diego in the bar that night and then killed Bianchi to silence him."

"Damn, I sure wish you guys had some hard evidence of this."

"You saw the photos I took that night."

"Yes, but I can't convict anyone with those alone."

- - - -

The next morning Bob used the privileges of his PI license to access state web sites to look into the finances of Maria Palumbo. He quickly discovered that Maria had an Arizona real estate broker license. On inspection of publicly available records, Bob saw that the Carmine Palumbo estate valuation was listed at the state tax revenue office at $3.8 million with property tax of $110,000 paid for the past year. There was no record of the financial account from which the payment was made. Bob decided that the information he was looking for, namely, financial tie-in between Maria and Rinaldi, was probably easier found by searching the Maria Palumbo trash bins on a regular basis. He would discuss the idea with Greg and see if he was up for it.

Greg listened to Bob describe his idea to retrieve Palumbo business and financial records from their trash bins on trash collection day.

"It's all legal, right?"

"Yep. Trash placed at the street for pickup is no longer considered private property."

"I hope you're right." Greg pulled out his cell phone. "I'll check with the city as to the trash pickup schedule where Maria lives."

When Greg put his phone away Bob asked, "Can you get a bunch of full trash bags in your car. It's not very big."

"That's true but I know a guy, Bruce, that'll give me a ride there in his pickup. He always needs money. I think a hundred bucks ought to do it."

Bob nodded. "That works for me. I'm concerned about you being up that way by yourself."

Greg grimaced. "No one will expect an old pickup with two guys in it, I hope."

"You know, I have this client that hasn't paid me for some title search I did for him. I'll give him a call and see about using his garage for few hours, maybe for a hundred bucks. We can spread out all the trash and sort through it."

Greg smiled. "That sure beats spreading all that crap out here in the office."

"I'm sure he's at work now. I'll give him a call after four."

"Okay. I'll catch up with you later. There's a couple of dead beats I want to check on."

The night before trash pickup, Greg and his friend, Bruce, drove by the Palumbo estate to scout for a safe time to empty the trash containers without being witnessed. They went back to the Palumbo property at 3am to empty the trash bins into the back of the pickup. Fortunately, all the trash had been placed in plastic trash bags. They drove to the garage that Bob had arranged to use in east Phoenix. The garage door had been opened and Bob stood there waiting for them.

They tossed the bags onto the concrete floor. Bob gave Bruce the agreed payment and he drove away in his pickup. Greg closed the overhead garage door, and then he and Bob sat on the floor and sorted through the trash. It was almost 8am when they completed the task. The selected trash items to be further checked for useful information were placed in a cardboard box while the rest of the trash was put back in the plastic bags. Bob placed the box in the trunk of the car. The trash bags were stuffed into the back seat. Bob placed a $100 bill on the garage floor as they left and shut the garage door. On the way back to the office Bob stopped at dumpsters where Greg tossed the trash bags.

Bob cleared the conference table for the contents of the cardboard box.

"What a pile of crap," grumbled Greg.

Bob nodded. "This may be a giant waste of time. Let's put stuff in separate piles, receipts, statements and bills. See if we can make anything out of all this."

They paid particular attention to monthly bills and receipts for electric power, the cable company, and the cell phone service provider. The account information was noted, but absent was the all-important checking account number of the payments.

Business letters and advertisements convinced Greg that Maria Palumbo was an active real estate broker. "Hey Bob, looks like she's a real estate broker."

"That's what I think also." Bob spent a few minutes on the smart phone and found a copy of Maria's business license. "Yep. She's a licensed broker."

Greg looked at Bob. "I've got a bill here for services from an accounting and tax preparation office. Maybe I should take a stab at breaking into the accountants file records. I've got some nifty software that can hide my identity."

Bob shook his head. "Not a good idea. Don't involve yourself in felonious activity."

Bob was able to access the Maricopa County property valuation and tax records and located information on the Palumbo Estate. Ownership was still shown as being Carmine Palumbo. It was a question whether Carmine's Last Will and Testament would benefit Maria in disposition of the property. Current valuation was $3M. The recent tax basis was $110K/year.

Bob searched for the Last Will and Testament of Carmine Palumbo but was unable to locate it in the state and county records accessible to him.

Greg found a receipt for the purchase of 5,000 shares of The Kraft Heinz Company issued by Merrill Lynch. Bob copied the account number to his record. It seemed certain from the torn up records that Maria and Carmine had separate checking and Visa accounts at the Valley Merchants Bank. Bob told Greg that normally a court order would be needed to investigate these accounts. They both agreed it would be important to acquire the contents of the Palumbo trash right after the bank and credit card statements were received. Greg said he would plan to do that.

The next morning Bob finished his coffee while he wondered what Rick Greene was up to. As a Palumbo soldier, was he also the primary hit man in the organization? Had he killed the Palumbo man having an affair with the FBI woman using a car bomb? How about the news reporter? Was Greene now a threat to Bob and Greg? What did Christy know about him?

Bob called Christy and she answered at her office.

"Hi Bob, I only have a few minutes."

"Just wondered what you had on Rick Greene. He's a regular fraudster, but what else is he?"

"Well, he's a piece of work, a regular soldier in the Palumbo outfit. He's suspected in some killings and the recent car explosions that you know about. Not a nice guy. We have bits and pieces but not enough to bring him in. Why do you ask?"

"I worry if I'm putting Greg in danger with this guy. He has to suspect he's being watched from time to time."

"You should worry. This guy is bad news. You and Greg are in danger from him."

"Okay. I'll have a talk with Greg."

"By the way, was your trash dive successful, or shouldn't I ask."

"Learned some things, but we need to do more."

"Okay. I heard enough. Just keep it legal."

"Will you be busy tonight?"

"I don't know yet. Stay outa trouble."

Christy disconnected.

Bob worried about the phone call. Christy had seemed short with him. He wondered if she was annoyed with his marginally legal antics. He cared about her and wished her the greatest success in her law enforcement career. He was troubled with the prospects of her moving further from him as they dealt with bringing justice for Laura and Carmine. In the meantime, he decided to head off trouble with Rick Greene and called Frank Palumbo.

"Hello."

"This is Bob Wagner. You have a minute?"

"Yeah. What's up?"

"I'm trying to head off trouble between you, me, my employee and Rick Greene."

"What the hell are you talking about?" he growled. "What trouble?"

"Frank, you know the kind of insurance investigation work I do here with the state and all. My guy Greg is a youngster who's doing a lot of footwork for me. We're certain Rick Greene knows that Greg has been on his tail about insurance fraud and child support. Before things get out of hand, I'd like to propose that you tell Greene to make full restitution on what he owes for child support payments. That way, we can stop shadowing him and the lawyers will relax, at least on that particular score."

"Boy, you got brass ones, I'll give you that."

"Just trying to avoid trouble…"

"Yeah, yeah. You're a royal pain in the ass, but I'll look into it. Are we done?"

"Thanks, Frank."

"Yeah, sure."

Bob placed the desk phone back on the cradle. There was a bead of sweat on his brow and he wiped at it with his fingers. He realized he had pushed his relationship with Frank about as far as he dared. But the thought of Greg in danger from the killer, Rick Greene, scared him. He called Greg.

"Hey, Bob. What's up?"

"You home?"

"Yep. Trying to catch up on things."

"Listen, Greg, I just had a few words with Frank Palumbo. I'd like you to back away from Greene for a while…until I can see if my suggestion to Frank pays off."

"Really? By the way, I haven't found where Greene has a regular job anywhere. It may be that he's doing, lets say, errands for some of the guys in the outfit. It's hard to get him for support payments if we can't find an employer."

"I think we know how he makes his money. I hope we can get this settled before Greene makes trouble. I worry about you out there."

"Okay, I'll back off. We're still looking at him for Workers Comp fraud, aren't we?"

"Yes, we are. But let it rest for a while. I worry about what the bastard will do when he gets pissed and sees you tailing him."

"Okay. I got it."

"Stay safe."

Bob put the phone down. Sure hope Frank comes through.

Four days later, Bob received a call from the law office of Morgan and Dunlop advising him that Rick Greene had brought his child support payments up to date and that Bob could discontinue his surveillance of their client in this regard. Bob was pleased to take some pressure off of Greg. He was particularly happy that Frank had respected his request.

CHAPTER 21

PAUL SALERNO

Christy received a call from Officer Anderson of the Phoenix PD.

"Hello Stuart. What's happening in Phoenix?"

"Same old stuff. I called because the dude you talked to a while back has been rearrested and is going to do a year at Florence. He said he wanted to talk to you before he left here. We don't have a problem with that if you're interested. Otherwise, we'll ship him out tomorrow."

"It's Salerno, right?"

"Yeah. Another drug charge."

"He wasn't real talkative last time."

"Yeah, well, it could be a waste of your time."

"Oh, what the heck. I'll be over early afternoon."

"See you then."

Stuart led Christy to a small conference room. Paul Salerno sat straight up in his chair with his wrists cuffed behind him.

"Can you unhook him?" asked Christy.

Stuart nodded to the guard who then removed the cuffs. Salerno proceeded to rub his wrists vigorously.

"Alright Salerno, make nice with the detective here."

Treachery | 107

Christy took a seat across from him at the table. "Mr. Salerno, why don't we start by you telling me what you know regarding Maria Palumbo and Tony Romano?"

"I drive them around when Romano calls me."

"You have the address and phone for Romano?"

He told Christy the address and phone number to Tony Romano's apartment.

"I'm not the only driver for those two. He changes around."

"Have you driven them to visit Carlos Rinaldi?"

He shook his head. "Never been there. He lives at the Biltmore Gardens in Tucson."

"How do you know this?"

"I overheard them talking about it when I drove them to the Skyline Club up in North Phoenix."

"Did you go inside the club?"

He shook his head again. "You kiddin'? Waited in the car. Musta been well over an hour."

"I understand Rinaldi brought in a couple of dudes from Boston. What do you know about them?"

"Just what I overheard. I never seen 'em."

"What was it you overheard?"

Salerno shifted in his chair. "You gonna be able to do anything for me?"

"I understand you've been sentenced to twelve months."

Salerno nodded. "It's a tough place."

"I'd be willing to make a recommendation, but you have to keep talking."

He rubbed his wrists again.

"The two guys are Nick Carlucci and Mike Agouti. I guess they're kinda famous…from the McFarland gang in Boston."

Christy was pleased to get confirmation of the two names she had heard before, but didn't let it show. "You pull these names out of your ass?"

Salerno looked offended. "No… I heard about them more than once. They're supposed to be specialists, according to the rumors, anyway."

"Why were these two specialists brought in? Do you know?"

He shook his head. "Never heard. But, Carmine Palumbo died that same week."

"There was a young woman hit that same day."

"Didn't hear about that."

"Other Palumbo people targeted?"

"Don't know. Romano and she never talked about what these two guys did. They talked a lot about their old lives in Chicago."

"Why was Carmine hit? What did you hear about that?"

"They never talked about it in the car. Bar room talk is mainly about how it helps Rinaldi. Rumor has it the Palumbo outfit will have to merge with Rinaldi soon."

"So, when Maria wanted to go somewhere she called you?"

"No. She had her own car, a silver Mercedes. But when she wanted to go see Tony, I'd get a call from his office telling me when to pick her up."

"Who else lives at the Palumbo estate?"

"I've never been inside. I stay in the car. She comes out and gets in and we go."

"No mention of anyone else?"

"She doesn't say much to me when we drive. She gets on her phone. It's always the same cars parked there."

"So, there's no one else in that big house?"

Salerno shrugged. "I never saw anyone else, but there's gotta be house keepers, I would think."

Christy folded her notebook and got up to leave. She turned to face him. "I will be making a recommendation. Thanks for your help."

Salerno nodded several times and Christy left the room.

The phone rang as Christy prepared to leave her desk the next afternoon.

"Hello. Holland."

"Christy, this is Stuart Anderson. Got some news you should hear."

"I don't need any bad news."

"Got a call from Florence. They tell me our boy Salerno was knifed to death in the exercise yard."

"Shit. He just got there. They have a suspect?"

"You know how that goes. No one saw a thing."

"Of course not. Thanks for the call."

"Take care."

CHAPTER 22

NICK CARLUCCI AND MICHAEL AGOUTI

Christy had asked the FBI for information on the two suspects identified by the late Paul Salerno. They had yet to respond. She called Bob to bring him up to date.

"Hi Christy, nice to hear from you. What's up?"

"Hey Bob, I had a little chat with one of Rinaldi's gophers. You know him, Paul Salerno. Too bad he's already dead."

"What happened to him?"

"He got knifed the same day he got to Florence."

"Interesting. What'd he have to say?"

"He told me the two suspects brought in from Boston by Rinaldi, presumably, were for the murder of Carmine. He didn't know who actually arranged to bring them in. But he identified the suspects as Nick Carlucci and Michael Agouti from the McFarland gang."

"Wow. This is progress. Appreciate your telling me."

"There's more. The PD here in Scottsdale spent hours reprocessing the images of the two men that assaulted you in that alley behind the restaurant. I heard they bought some state-of-the-art software. Anyway, I don't know how, but they now have a high degree of confidence that these two guys are the same two suspects in the Carmine/Laura killing."

"This is great news. But it's not 100 percent yet?"

"No, not good enough yet. DA is hesitant to arrest the two men, as no direct evidence exists. The DA posited any lawyer could get them free with minimum bail, and then they would likely flee the jurisdiction or even the country."

After a few days, Bob felt better and the pain in his arm was manageable with common medication. He and Greg decided to do another raid on Maria Palumbo's trash. It was after midnight when they stopped by the trash containers at the Palumbo estate. They looked around but saw no one watching. A few minutes later, a Scottsdale PD vehicle pulled up behind them with the light bar flashing. A single officer got out of his car and approached the driver's side and stopped just behind Bob's shoulder.

"What are you doing here, sir?"

"Picking up trash. It's not illegal."

"Uh-huh. Hand me your driver's license."

Bob reached to his back pocket for his wallet.

"I just want to grab the trash bags and be on my way."

"Why are you doing this?"

"I'm an investigator." Bob handed the officer a business card with his license. "I'm investigating."

"No kidding? A gen-u-ine investigator? Wow."

"It's what I do."

"Not today, Dick Tracy. Residents here don't want anyone rummaging in their trash. So, move along." He handed the license back.

Bob nodded and started the engine. The officer stepped back. Bob drove away and headed back to his office. Greg had remained silent but now voiced his exasperation. "I think it's the same cop that hassled me the other week. What's the big deal?"

"We didn't find anything very useful last time. This time they were forewarned, so it's not likely they would have left anything useful in the trash."

Greg nodded. "I have to agree. We didn't strike gold last time."

When Bob arrived at his office the next morning, he parked his car in the usual spot under the shade awning at the rear of the building. As he walked toward the rear entrance, a dark luxury car drove up and blocked his path. The back door opened and a well-dressed man got out. He motioned for Bob to get in, emphasizing his request with a movement of his hand in his jacket pocket, suggestive of a pistol.

Bob sat in the luxurious air-conditioned comfort of the Mercedes and slid to the other side as the man gestured and got in and closed the door. The cool air was agreeable. The view of the driver and passenger was obscured by a screen and dark glass. The glass was suddenly lowered leaving only the screen in the opening. No one spoke for many seconds, and then Bob heard who he thought was the passenger speaking. He was unable to see the driver or the passenger.

"Am I speaking to Bob Wagner?"

"Yes. Who the hell are you?"

"I'm going to ask you a question. Are you listening?"

"Yeah."

"What is your interest in annoying Mrs. Palumbo and her friends?"

"Annoying? I'm investigating...as allowed by law."

"You're investigating on whose behalf?"

"No one is paying me. I do not have a client."

There was a few seconds pause.

"You've been meddling in the business of Mrs. Palumbo. Namely, prowling in her trash, leaving footprints on county computer records, and sending someone dumpster diving to further annoy Mrs. Palumbo and her friends."

There was another pause.

"Are you going to deny this?"

"No. I was doing what I had to do, while keeping within the law."

"And what is it that you had to do? What exactly are you after?"

"Someone murdered Carmine. I want to know who the two thugs were."

"Two thugs?"

"A witness described to several people, two thugs coming out of Carmine's room."

"Sounds like something for the police."

"They also murdered a witness, a young lady…a friend of mine."

"Sad, but what does all this have to do with Mrs. Palumbo and her friends?"

"It all started with why Carmine was murdered. It all devolved from that."

"Like I said, what does it have to do with Mrs. Palumbo or her friends?"

"One can postulate that Rinaldi would benefit significantly by Carmine's removal. Also, it's possible the two thugs were imported from Boston to eliminate Carmine and make the growth of the Rinaldi outfit in the Phoenix area much easier."

After a few seconds pause, "That's an interesting hypothesis. Are you going to expand on this in your next Op-Ed?"

"It seems that the death of Carmine isn't getting a lot of press or police attention. Be that as it may. The murder of the witness, a young woman and friend of mine, will continue to get serious investigative attention until the two criminals are arrested and convicted and whoever ordered the killing is prosecuted."

"You work for the Gazette? Is that it?"

"No. But they will get the full story."

"You have no call to stir up all this trouble on your unsupported suppositions."

"It's my opinion Rinaldi's people and Maria Palumbo have their prints all over this."

"Neither Mrs. Palumbo nor her friends had anything to do with the tragedy you speak of. You're causing a lot of anxiety with your lawful meddling in other people's lives."

"I'm an investigator. It's what I do. I get to the bottom of things."

"You'll get to the bottom of a mine shaft, that's what you'll get." The man's voice had hardened. "Your meddling and harassment will come at a very real price. Now, get the fuck out of the car."

Bob opened the door and got out quickly. He pushed the door closed and the car moved away. The license plate showed a livery permit and he memorized the four digits. Sweat soaked his armpits and trickled down the side of his face.

Up in his office, Bob took his pistol from the holster hanging on a coat hook, checked it, and placed it in the front drawer of his desk. He had never had to shoot anyone, but he now realized his inquiries and those of the Scottsdale PD were making some people anxious and angry. It seemed no one cared much about finding Carmine's killer as the story had disappeared from the news in less than a week. The murder of Laura had disappeared from the TV news after two days. However, Bob wasn't going to stop trying to get Laura's murderer brought to justice. The incident had saddened and sickened him as he had come to care about her in the short time he knew her.

He picked up his phone and called Christy.

"Hi Bob, What's up?"

"Wanted to hear your voice."

"I'd rather it be in person."

"Me too, but I wanted to tell you of an interesting meeting I had today."

"Really? Who with?"

"Well, that's just it. Let me tell you. I was walking from my car to this building a few minutes ago. A black limo pulled up between the building and me. A well dressed guy gets out of the back and tells me to get in."

"He was armed?"

"The dude had his hand in his jacket pocket indicating a gun. I didn't argue with him. I got in the back and he slid in next to me. I couldn't see the people in the front. There was a mesh screen at the window. Anyway, it was the passenger who spoke."

"Okay…"

"The guy started out by asking me what my interest was in annoying Mrs. Palumbo and her friends."

"No clue to who was speaking?"

"I couldn't place the voice. He wanted to know just why I was looking into the affairs of Maria Palumbo and her friends and who was paying me. He asked if I was doing this for a newspaper. I said no one was paying me; that I wanted to know who the killer of Laura was and by association, the killer of Carmine. There was some more back and forth."

"Damn," Her voice had a surprising edge. "You just had to shoot your mouth off to this guy?"

"He was getting angry. Guy said I was going to end up at the bottom of a mine shaft."

"And you have no clue who he was?"

"I assumed it was one of the Rinaldi guys, maybe Romano."

"Or the man himself."

"I don't know."

"You need to be a lot more careful." Her voice was stern. "Quit shooting your mouth off. You just got a warning. There won't be another."

"I can't give up on this. By the way, I have the livery tag number." He read it off to her.

"Hang on a second. I'm looking it up…Yep. I got it. That tag is a stolen plate."

"Of course it is."

"Bob…no real evidence exists yet in the murder of Carmine and Laura. Nothing that the DA can use to pursue arrest warrants. If we grab the two suspects we've identified for the assault on Greg and from the description Laura gave you, they'd be out on bail the next day and disappear."

"I know. I have to be a lot more careful now. But I'm not giving up on this."

"I promise this will be pursued every chance we get here at the PD."

"I love you."

"I know you do."

Christy hung up.

CHAPTER 23

WHAT NOW?

Bob and Greg discussed the likelihood of a violent intruder being sent to silence Bob for his public accusations that imply Rinaldi responsibility for the murder of Carmine and Laura.

"Christ, Bob, some bad-ass could walk right in here and blow you away."

Bob nodded. "I guess I better tighten this place up."

"At least put in some cameras and an electronic door lock. You still have your piece here in the office?"

"Yeah. Top drawer of my desk."

"How about I go buy a couple cameras and a digital recorder? I'll install the recorder in the coat closet."

"Okay. Pick up what you need for an electronic door lock. Make it so I can work it from my desk."

"No problem." Greg held out his hand. "Pony over your credit card."

Bob pulled out his wallet. "Keep the cost down."

"Okay. I'll be back in a couple hours."

"So how are we going to do this?" Bob looked at the receipt with a scowl.

Greg was pulling things out of a cardboard box. "I was thinking of putting two of these motion activated cameras in your office and one out here in the outer area."

"What about this recording equipment?"

"I checked out the coat closet in the hallway and the shelf in there is perfect for the digital video recorder. I'll have to run cables and power cords."

"I sure hope this is worth what it's going to cost me." Bob looked at the receipt again.

"I have this special door lock and a special switch for your desk. This is a wireless setup. It's a little pricy but it avoids putting in long wires."

Bob shook his head. "Okay. I sure hope it works."

"Not to worry. I'll have this working by evening."

As Greg worked to install the equipment at the door and the cameras, Bob tried to put his mind on the financial statements from the bank. However, his thoughts were interrupted as he wondered if Greene was acting at Frank Palumbo's direction and they planed to avenge Carmine's murder by eliminating the two Boston shooters. But on the other hand, if Greene had contracted to have the two shooters brought in from Boston on the direction of Rinaldi, then Greene was hiding in plain sight with Palumbo people. Bob felt the situation was unstable and would have to come to some end soon.

Bob wanted to see the two shooters arrested and prosecuted for the two murders. Only then would he feel any sense of justice for Laura. If someone in the Palumbo outfit revenge-killed the two shooters, he would be denied the justice he craved. He had to find the two suspects and have them arrested before Frank had them killed; or alternatively, before Greene had them killed to protect his own culpability.

- - - -

Late in the afternoon, Christy stopped at the hotel where Carmine was murdered to again inspect the images from the camera at the end of the hallway from which Laura had come and another camera at the elevator and exit stairs past Carmine's room. The recordings were stored in a server in a small room behind the main desk. The images clearly showed the two men entering as well as leaving Carmine's room, but the facial features had been obscured by full-face masks. Christy had then discovered the camera in the front lobby still had images saved of the two men at the day in question. Color images from this camera clearly showed the masked faces of the two presumed hit men. No identifying features were evident to her. She gave the image recordings to the forensics laboratory at the PD in the hope they could, with their new software, enhance any identifying features.

- - - -

The apparent success of the Rinaldi outfit in Tucson had encouraged the aging Carmine, a long time Chicago resident, to start a branch of the Palumbo outfit in Scottsdale. The idea of pleasant weather and calmer environs pleased him. Frank Palumbo realized he had lost some of his crew after Carmine had been murdered. Several had returned to their old haunts in Chicago. Carmine had been a strong and respected leader of the outfit and he had discouraged members from dealing in drugs. With the dissatisfaction and fracture now in the outfit, Frank assumed some members would no longer be loyal. There had been vocal opposition to the no-drugs policy as this prevented members profiting in the lucrative trade. Frank, feeling control of the group slipping away, was anxious to ferret out traitors and deal with them. He wanted to understand the Rinaldi involvement with the Carmine killing. It didn't make a lot of sense to him, as Carmine was by then only a figurehead. It would have made more sense for someone to target himself instead. He had to know what had happened. He knew he didn't have the muscle any longer or leverage to force Rinaldi's hand. Also, he would have to assess the amount of Rinaldi drug infiltration into the Phoenix area and develop a plan to counter it. He was only now beginning to see a serious profit from drug sales in his own outfit. He'd have to do the investigative work by himself and quietly until he could make a move.

"Then there's the pain-in-the-ass PI, Wagner," he mumbled to himself. That meddling fool is soft in the head and could inadvertently make trouble for me with his crusade to avenge the babe's murder. Shit, I can't afford to have Wagner stir up trouble with my own men, not now with the outfit in disarray.

Bastard is also causing a real dust up in the Rinaldi outfit, he thought. He has that cop babe whispering in his ear. Wonder what she knows about the murder of my uncle? I've got to have an understanding with him, gotta set some rules, maybe even today. The crazy bastard is going to get himself killed for sure at this rate. Frank was annoyed with himself at being fond of the PI, ever since the guy had helped him out of a jam. But that had been a while ago. He looked at his watch.

Yep, still time to pay the dude a visit. Frank got out of his chair, made a call to Dino, and then headed out to his car. He didn't expect trouble, not from Wagner, but just in case, Dino was the man to bring along.

- - - -

Greg had just left for the day and Bob meditated at his desk, worrying that the Rinaldi people wanted to prevent him from testifying at an upcoming grand jury regarding the murder of Carmine. Startled, he looked up as the door burst open and two men barged into the outer office hurling invectives. Bob reached into his desk drawer and pulled out his pistol. As the men came to his private office there was gunfire. The window behind Bob shattered. Wounded in the upper left arm, he blindly returned two shots as he dove off his chair to drop behind his desk. Pain and fear gripped him in panic as he pressed his wound with his right hand to slow the bleeding. Then he heard more gunshots seemingly from outside the office.

- - - -

Frank and Dino had driven into the front parking area of the office building. As Frank parked, Dino pointed to two casually dressed men about to enter the building.

"Hey! I know those bastards! Son of a bitch! They're Romano's guys!"

"Oh shit. Dino they're after Wagner. Go get 'em!"

Dino burst from the car and sprinted toward the building entrance.

Seconds later Frank was out of the car and running toward Dino. "Get 'em, Dino!"

Frank and Dino rushed into the building and scampered up the stairs to the second floor. They could hear men's voices yelling above them. As they reached the second floor loud gunfire echoed down the hallway.

Dino forcibly pushed past Frank toward the office door. "Lemme in there!"

Frank pulled the pistol from his back and approached the office door as a loud volley of shots filled the air. Frank stood at the doorway and saw two men lying on the floor at the doorway to the inner office. They were nearly on top of each other. Dino leaned against the wall in the outer office with a hand clamped against a bloody wound in his side.

"What the hell happened here? Where's Bob? Jesus, you're hit!"

- - - -

Bob in pain and frightened pulled his cell phone from his pocket with his right hand and dialed 9-1-1. He managed a short message before dropping the phone. He heard his name being yelled.

"Bob! Shit! Where the hell are you?"

"Who?"

"It's Frank, goddamnit! Where the hell are you?"

"Over here… Behind the desk."

Bob heard heavy footsteps and looked up to see Frank looking down at him.

"I called 9-1-1," gasped Bob.

"Yeah, yeah. How bad you hurt? Can you get up? Holy shit!"

Bob grabbed Frank's extended arm and was pulled up to sit in his desk chair.

"Where ya hit? Just your arm? Where else?"

"Yeah, my arm. Fuckin' hurts… What the hell happened?"

"Shit. You tell me. Dino and I saw those guys come in the building. Knew there'd be trouble and then heard shots."

"Two guys stormed in here…"

"Yeah, Dino took care of them. He got hit too."

"Who the hell were those two?"

"They're Romano guys. Shit, I hear cops coming."

"Lots of trouble now."

"Yeah…here they come."

Things were in a blur for Bob. Police arrived, then two more and then the EMTs. Bob tried to answer questions from the police but he felt everything slipping away.

Bob awoke to see his arm heavily bandaged and an IV drip in his other arm. The pain was dull but not to be ignored. Daylight was seeping in through the closed drapes. He wondered if it was still the same day. He tried to recall all that had happened, but he had lost track after the police arrived. When the door opened, he saw Christy standing there shaking her head.

She came to him and kissed him. "Jesus, Bob, you stepped into it now, didn't you?"

"Was it today?"

"A few hours ago." She pulled a recorder and notebook from her pocket. "I have to get a statement from you. Might as well do it now. So, what the hell happened?"

"Frank…?"

Christy nodded. "Talked to him. Got him locked up for now. Talked to that Dino guy, too. He's in here…took one in the side…lucky he had all that blubber."

"Greg and I put in some cameras…"

"I talked to Greg. He gave me the video."

"Should show everything."

"Sorry. I know you're uncomfortable right now. But I need to get your statement."

"Okay." Bob took a deep breath. "Sitting at my desk thinking. Two guys burst into the outer office. I reached into my desk for my gun. I think that's when the first guy shot and missed me and broke my window. As I raised my pistol, I was hit. I dove to the floor behind my desk. I did manage to get off a couple shots. I pulled my phone out of my pocket and dialed 9-1-1."

"There were two dead bodies in your office. You were wounded and this Dino guy was wounded. And then there was Frank. What the hell were he and this Dino dude doing there?"

"When I dove behind my desk, I heard shooting and shouting in the outer office. Then Frank came in and helped me get into my chair. Then the cops came. I don't recall much after that."

"What the hell was Frank doing there?" insisted Christy.

"We never got to talk. I don't think he said. Didn't you talk to him?"

"Yep. I have his statement. But right now, I just want to hear it from you. Is there anything else to add?"

Bob shook his head.

Christy pocketed her recorder and her notebook. She stood next to him and smiled. "I'm glad you're going to be okay. I don't know why, but I still love you." She kissed him.

At the door she turned to him. "Greg is out here. I'll send him in."

"Bob, for crisakes, I'm sure glad you're going to be okay." Greg came over to Bob's bed. "I couldn't believe it when Christy called me. She had to tell me twice."

"Yeah, I've had better days."

"Who the hell shot you?"

"One of those dead guys."

"Well, who shot them? You?"

"I fired off a couple shots as I dove behind my desk. Don't know if I hit anyone. I think Frank's guy shot them both."

"Lucky for you. What was he doing there?"

"Don't know. I never got to talk to him."

"He saved your ass."

"Yeah. You could put it that way."

"Christy said she has Frank in jail."

"Yeah, she has protocol to follow. Frank's guy is in this hospital, bullet in his side."

"Jesus, what happens now?"

"I have to talk to my attorney. Lots of legal bullshit to deal with."

"Why didn't you have your door locked? We put in that fancy lock and a switch on your freakin' desk."

"Forgot all about it. But I'll remember from now on."

"Is Christy pissed at you?"

"She's not happy."

Greg brought Bob back to his office in the afternoon of the next day. Bob had his left arm in a sling and he sat at his desk with a bottle of pain pills and a large Dunkin' Donuts coffee.

"I can come by later. I have a stakeout to do when it gets dark. You going to be okay for a while?"

"Yeah. I'll be okay here. I got my coffee…that's important."

"You've got to keep the damn door locked. Some badass comes, it gives you a chance to get ready and to call 9-1-1."

"Yeah, yeah. Go on, get the hell outa here. Stay safe."

Greg waved and left. Bob pushed the switch on his desk and he heard the lock click shut.

An hour later, he was surprised to hear several loud knocks. He hesitated to unlock the door.

"Hey! Open the damn door! This is Frank!"

Bob reached for the door switch. There was a loud click and Frank swung the door open.

"Hey Frank."

Frank grinned. "I'm not gonna get shot, am I?"

"No. But I want to thank you for your help yesterday."

"Yeah, yeah. Lucky break. I'd say we're even now. Don't you think?"

Bob nodded several times. "I don't know why you were there, but I'm grateful."

"Your lady cop said I'm on a short leash, but she let me go for now after I came up with a shit-load of bail."

"Your man still in the hospital?"

"Yeah. A couple more days. I don't know about bail for him…maybe."

Bob pointed to a chair in front of his desk and Frank sat down. He turned the chair to be able to see the office door.

"Listen to me, Bob. I want to know what you know…as fact…about Maria's relationship with Rinaldi and this Tony Romano guy. I want facts and no bullshit."

Bob rubbed his chin and cleared his throat. "My main interest from day one has been to get some justice for the senseless murder of Laura. I'm sorry about your uncle's death and of course his murder is what started this. Laura was a witness. She described what she saw to Gina and me. Is that enough to put the shooters behind bars? I don't know. I kept wondering if your guys would make the two shooters disappear and then there wouldn't be any justice for Laura…in my opinion. I knew I had to find out who the two guys were and get them arrested before they vanished or your guys got to them."

"Yeah, well, that's all very interesting, but you're not answering my question. Let's get to it."

"I figured in order to know who the shooters were I'd have to find out why Carmine was killed. Who would benefit from Carmine's death? Was it his wife? Was it his nephew? Was it both of them?"

A scowl came over Frank's face. "What the hell…?"

Bob held up his hand. "I couldn't see where you would benefit as Carmine already had you running things. I couldn't come up with an enemy now that Carmine was not in the day-to-day business. So I decided that we needed to look a little deeper into what Maria was up to. There had to be a reason to murder Carmine…and therefore Laura."

"Oh for crisakes, get to it!"

"We started looking into all aspects of Maria's life; business, real estate, banking and her private life. We got solid information of a relationship between her and Rinaldi going back to Chicago. When she moved here some years back, she latched onto Carmine. Not long after that she became close with Tony Romano, a Rinaldi guy." Bob paused and took a deep breath.

"We saw video clearly showing the two masked killers at the door to Carmine's room at the hotel and at the registration desk. Recently, I've been warned off of looking at the Maria, Romano, and Rinaldi connection. I can't identify them, but I'm pretty sure now it was Romano doing the talking. I'd bet Romano sent those two bastards here the other day. I'll be doing what I can with the Scottsdale PD to grab the two killers and have them indicted."

"Marvelous. And the bottom line is what?"

"I have to assume at this point that Maria is working with Rinaldi so he can take over the Palumbo outfit here in Arizona. I think killing Carmine was but a step in that direction."

Frank was silent, his fingers tented at his mouth. About twenty seconds passed before he spoke, still in the thoughtful pose. "What is it you want?"

"I would like to have the two Carmine shooters arrested and prosecuted for Laura's murder. If they were to be prosecuted for Carmine's murder it would be after they were tried for killing Laura."

Frank shifted in his chair and shook his head. "My uncle was murdered. That's not the way we do things. Those two have to be taken out."

"I'd like to have them tried for Laura's murder first."

"I let you do that and what? Maybe they go to prison, and then where am I? My people expect certain justice for Carmine. I give you what you want and I'll look like a fuckin' pussy."

"Suppose we indict them for both murders and try them together?" said Bob. "Maybe the DA would go for it."

"And what do I tell my people? For crisakes, the trial could be a couple years out. No, I can't afford to look like a fuckin' wimp. I have enough troubles to deal with."

"I can't condone what you're thinking to do."

"I give a rat's ass what you think?" The muscles in Frank's face tightened.

Both men paused and fell silent for a minute.

"Alright, no one goes after those two right now," said Frank. "You get them arrested and locked up right away; it'll get me off the hook. Otherwise, after a couple weeks it'll be all over for those two."

Bob shook his head slowly.

"That's the way its gonna be! Work with it!" Frank, his face dark, got out of the chair and turned to Bob. "We're not talking about this anymore." Frank walked through the office and out into the corridor.

The office door closed behind him and Bob heard the loud click of the lock as he pushed the switch.

CHAPTER 24
EVIDENCE

Bob's phone rang several times before he picked it up.

"Hi Christy."

"Bob how are you? It's been a couple days."

"I'm at my desk. Haven't got much enthusiasm this morning."

"I'm sorry. I guess you're still in some pain."

"I'm very sore. I've got a bottle of ibuprofen and a large coffee. What's new?"

"I need you to tell me again what happened at your office. I need to make sure I have it all down correctly."

"Do we have to? I mean I've been all over it."

"Should I call later?"

Bob let out a long sigh. "Let's just do it."

"You said a man came into your outer office and fired a gun at you, breaking your window."

"Two guys came into my office. The guy in front showed a gun. I reached for my pistol in the desk drawer and that's when he fired. The shot went through the window."

"Okay. Then what?"

"As he fired the second shot, I was just diving behind my desk. The shot hit my arm."

"You said you grabbed your pistol and dove to the floor. You fired the pistol?"

"Yes. Twice. I don't know if I hit them or not. I called 9-1-1 from the floor."

"There were two?" she asked.

"Yes, two. I already said that."

"So now you're behind the desk…"

"Yes. On the floor. I wasn't making sense of it. I was bleeding and it hurt a lot. I heard more shooting."

"Then you heard Frank Palumbo calling – shouting for you?"

"Yes. He found me behind the desk. Said his guy, Dino, shot the two guys coming for me," said Bob.

"Yeah, Joseph Ferrara and Michael Salvini. Tucson PD says they're low level Rinaldi guys," said Christy. "They have some history in Chicago."

"Someone sent them…maybe Romano."

"Doesn't make sense to me. Why two shooters? Why any shooters?"

"I know I'm not very popular with some people…but two shooters? Damn."

"It's over the top. I think shooting you at all is way too much. Doesn't make sense to me."

"Scared the crap outa me."

Christy shook her head. "Why was Frank there? It's rather curious, him getting there just in time."

"Back then, I had no idea. The cops and EMTs arrived. We didn't talk."

"So…did you hear from him?"

"He came by here earlier. I thanked him for helping me out."

"Yeah, he sure did."

"Anyhow, what he had wanted was to talk to me about what I thought was fact about Maria and Rinaldi and Tony Romano. I gave him a brief summary of what I thought I knew. I don't think I told him anything he didn't already know or suspect. He asked me what I wanted to get out of all this poking around I was doing."

"He asked you that?"

"Yep. So I let him know I wanted the killers of Laura arrested and in jail. That I was sorry about the death of Carmine, but I wanted justice for Laura."

"And then what?"

"His idea of justice for Carmine was to have the two killers whacked. But I told him that would deny me the chance of getting justice for Laura. He basically said he didn't care about that, as his people expected him to do justice for Carmine."

"It doesn't sound like he was impressed with your argument."

"He said something about my being a pussy. As he left, he said he'd give me two weeks to get the killers in jail; otherwise, things were going to go his way."

Christy shook her head. "Well…it's not up to you to put anyone in jail. The police and DA do that."

"I know. You think the PD can get those guys behind bars? You have the video from the hotel and my second hand witness statement. Can you work with that?"

"That's pretty damn weak. Even if we could find them and arrest them, a first year lawyer would have them out on bail by the end of the day."

"I should what, just give up?"

"I'm willing to push on the DA to indict them. But it's not likely to happen without some concrete evidence. The video is impressive but the DA will want more. They don't want to lose the case in court."

"Can you start the ball rolling? Assume the evidence will come."

Christy's voice hardened. "I told you…we don't have enough to hold them. Besides, we haven't located them. Rinaldi may move them around. Or, they may have skipped the state."

"I'll see if I can find them."

"No! Damn it, Bob! We can't hold them with what we got."

"If Frank finds them, it'll be too late!"

"Don't get yourself killed," said Christy, her voice softer. "I love you. I want you to remember that."

"I miss you."

"Me too. Bye."

Two days later, Christy arranged for Bob, Gina and her to meet with the assistant DA, Ronald Groveland, to discuss the evidence available regarding the murder of Carmine and Laura. Christy cautioned Bob to not expect the DA would agree to their very thin evidence. Instead, they could lay the groundwork to try again with the eventual recovery of additional evidence.

At the meeting, Bob talked about Laura spending an evening with him and telling him what she had experienced. Gina mentioned that Laura had spent time with her that day and they had discussed her situation. Christy showed the DA the hotel videos near the Carmine room and at the hotel entrance and registration desk.

The video showed masked men coming out of Carmine's room at the time of the murder. It also showed Laura approaching Carmine's room at the time of the murder with the same hit men in the photo as they left the room. It is evident in photos that the hit men saw Laura at that time and turned toward her, before being intimidated by an approaching group of guests and quickly exiting.

Christy presented a statement from the bartender at the hotel lounge that corroborated Laura being at the hotel at the time of the murder of Carmine and of her telling him she had received no response from

Carmine's room. Inspection of Laura's cell phone record showed her calling Carmine without getting a reply at the time of the murder. They offered the DA a statement of Laura's story in a sworn testament by Bob and Gina. The next day Christy was told the grand jury declined to indict the two suspects for the murder of Laura citing lack of sufficient evidence. They did, however, agree to an indictment in the murder of Carmine, but offered no explanation.

The following day, Christy received an okay from the DA to arrest the two suspected hit men, but only for the murder of Carmine. The suspects were described as Nick Carlucci and Michael Agouti. Christy read of their affiliation with the McFarland gang of Boston. The DA emphasized the evidence against the two suspects was thin. The main issue was that no video in the hotel captured an image of the perpetrators without their masks. There was no forensic identification. The DA said a judge would likely let them walk on moderate bail. Christy planned on keeping surveillance on the suspects if they were out on bail.

Scottsdale PD arrested the two hit men as they left the His & Hers Club. They were arraigned the next day and plead Not Guilty to the murder of Carmine. Bail was set at $500K each. Trial was set for 60 days hence, a speedy trial date agreed to by both parties due to danger of the suspects being assassinated. However, The DA said he would press the prosecutor for an even earlier trial, as the threat of assassination was very real.

- - - -

Bob met with Christy in his office to propose a new theory of the Carmine and Laura murders. Christy was skeptical and impatient with Bob's crusade, but with a shrug of her shoulders agreed to hear Bob's new ideas.

"I've been thinking, the Carmine murder and thus the Laura murder could be a secret plot devised by Rick Greene using killers he knew from Boston."

"Wow." Christy did an eye roll and shook her head. "Really?"

"Let's just suppose Greene becomes very dissatisfied with the operation and the rewards of the Palumbo outfit under the control of Carmine and the management by Frank Palumbo."

"Again with the Rick Greene thing?"

Bob nodded and continued undaunted. "His angst might well be based on disallowance by Carmine to trafficking in very lucrative narcotics sales. This prohibition and loss of related income may have possibly convinced Greene to join with some of the Rinaldi people in their effort to infiltrate and subsequently absorb the Palumbo outfit in Arizona, and to afford him an important position. The Rinaldi outfit is known to be the primary importer and supplier of meth and cocaine in southern Arizona."

Christy dropped her mocking grin, looked at Bob, and shook her head. "Is there any proof of this…any at all?"

"Hang on to that thought. I'm thinking there is huge risk to Rinaldi if he and Greene were to set up a hit on Carmine and be found out. However, an ambitious Rick Greene could mitigate the risk if he were to set up the whole operation by himself while inside the Palumbo organization. If that failed, Rinaldi could of course still continue his efforts to stir dissatisfaction in the Palumbo ranks in Arizona."

"Again with the Greene thing…and where are you going with this off-the-wall theory?"

"I wanted to get your thoughts on it."

"Uh-huh and then?"

"I'd like to bring up this theory to Frank and gage his response."

Christy shook her head. "I'll likely find you in a dumpster somewhere."

"You don't like the idea?"

"Surprisingly, it's an interesting theory. However, no evidence exists to support your theory. None. And, how's Frank going to react? How're you going to convince him?"

"Not sure I can. But if Frank accepted the idea, he could make it possible for the PD to obtain the evidence needed to pursue arrests and prosecutions of the killers."

"Yes…but this scares me. Even if your theory is correct, I'm fearful of how Frank would react." Christy shook her head. "He's a gangster after all."

Bob knew she was right.

- - - -

The next morning Bob placed a call to Frank to run his theory about Greene by him, hoping for some hint of a positive response.

"Yeah, Bob. What is it now?"

"Frank, I have an idea that I've been thinking more and more about and I'd like to run it by you. You think we could meet where we wouldn't be overheard?"

He heard Frank sigh. "I'm busy right now. Why don't you just tell me on the phone?"

"I'll wait until you're not so busy. I need to sit with you and talk about it."

"Oh for crisakes, I'll be at your office at ten this morning."

"Thanks, Frank."

"Yeah."

CHAPTER 25
THE MEETING

Bob heard Frank's heavy fist bang on the door. "Hey! Open up. It's Frank." Bob flipped the door switch.

Frank strode into the office dressed in casual clothes, but wearing a blue blazer. He took a seat in front of Bob's desk, turning the chair to be able to see the door.

"Lock that damn door, will ya?"

Bob flipped the door switch and they heard the lock click shut.

Frank looked at Bob, shook his head and said, "Alright, I'm here. Don't waste my time. Get on with it."

"I appreciate your coming here. What I'm going to say is only a theory. I'm not trying to piss you off, just hoping you'll hear me out."

"Yeah, yeah. Christ, you gonna tell me or what?"

"I'm thinking more and more that the hit on Carmine was not a direct Rinaldi operation. I cannot see where Rinaldi would take that risk since Carmine wasn't running things anymore. Yes, he still wanted Carmine gone and probably you, too, so he could get to his goal sooner of absorbing the Palumbo operation in Arizona. That way, he could greatly expand his narco distribution network in a bloodless coup, if he pulled it off."

"Uh-huh. Very interesting. Is there more to this theory of yours?" Frank drummed his fingers on the armrest.

Treachery | 137

"It's fairly common knowledge you're dealing with a lot of dissatisfaction in your organization, most of it from the lack of earnings by members since Carmine's edict that drug sales would not be part of doing business."

"Now, wait a damn minute…"

Bob raised his palm and Frank grimaced, but stayed silent.

"One of your most effective, productive and dedicated members has been Rick Greene. I've had to study him quite a bit since I've been contracted to report to the state agencies on his behavior as an insurance fraudster. I'm pretty sure he's taken care of some situations lately for you. But what I'm thinking, and this is only a theory, is that Greene is now in the Rinaldi camp."

"You're fuckin' crazy…" Frank's face turned dark.

"Just a minute, Frank. My idea is that Greene used two shooters that he knew from Boston to have the hit done on Carmine, and they killed Laura because she could possibly identify them. I think this operation, if not actually sanctioned, probably guaranteed Greene good standing with Rinaldi. As a strong soldier, he would be very useful to Rinaldi in expanding his narco operations."

"This is your fuckin' theory?"

"I was hoping you'd hear me out and we'd talk about it."

"Talk about it? I ought to rip your fuckin' throat out, you disrespectful prick!"

"Frank, I uh…"

"Where the hell you get off, coming up with this bullshit?"

"I …"

"You got some brass balls, I'll give you that."

"I thought a lot about…"

Frank stared at the floor while shaking his head. "Rick Greene? My top man?" He looked at Bob. "That's what you're sayin'?"

"It's a theory, Frank. Just trying to make sense of all that's happening."

"So you won't be insulted if I say you're full of shit?"

"I just kept thinking…why would Rinaldi risk it, even though he wanted Carmine gone? Then I thought of the dissatisfaction I kept hearing about, and the more I thought about it, it dawned on me that Rick Greene would be the perfect agent to pull it off. I can't prove any of this, but it's a theory I think worthy of some serious thought."

Frank's voice had softened. "You do, do you? Serious thought, huh?"

"Frank, I'm not trying to insult you…"

"Why the hell you telling me this?"

"I think you're in some danger. I…"

"Bullshit. What are you gonna get out of this?"

"Well, I was hoping you'd want the shooters indicted."

"Yeah? And Greene? What does your theory say about him?"

"I'm thinking he's the instigator. He should be indicted for this."

"No shit? You got it all figured out?"

"Frank, I…"

"First, I don't give a shit about your indictments."

"I know, it's…"

"Second, if I thought what you said was true, I would be looking to make some immediate changes."

"Frank, I don't wish harm to you. I'm looking for a measure of justice for Laura. But I think my theory could be right, and if it is there might be danger for you. I wanted you to hear me out and take me serious."

"Lately, I've been suspicious of everybody. But I just don't believe what you're saying about Greene. He's been a stand-up guy."

"I know from his history, he's been doing a lot of work on your behalf."

"Yeah, so?"

"It means also that he knows a lot about the Palumbo organization, the way things are done."

"So what?"

"If he turns against you, he could be valuable to Rinaldi…or to the feds if they grab him."

"So, what is it you're after? Why are you busting my balls? Let's hear it."

"Can't we prove it, one way or the other, about Greene?"

"Why?"

"If he set up the hit on Carmine, don't you want to know?"

"Of course."

"If he did it, wouldn't it be to benefit Rinaldi…and himself…not you…his boss?"

"This is your fuckin' theory?"

"Will you at least think about it? Play the whole scenario in your head."

Frank got out of the chair, his face dark. He shook his head. "One thing about you; you've always had a pair of brass ones…along with a big fuckin' mouth."

Bob watched Frank storm out of the office. Had he accomplished anything, he wondered, or had Frank turned against him?

CHAPTER 26
INDICTMENTS AND TRIAL

Frank parked behind Bruno's Pizza and went into the back room. It was a place where he felt comfortable, where he could think and be sure the weekly scouring for hidden electronic spying gadgets was keeping the place safe. Frank was angry with Bob. He had restrained himself from the urge to smash the face of the impudent bastard. Bob had stirred up turmoil that he certainly didn't need at this time. The outfit was decimated; Frank was keeping a low profile until he could build it back up. But now Frank found himself thinking often about Rick Greene. Rick seemed like a standup guy and he produced the most income in the outfit. Frank wondered how Bob arrived at the idea that Greene might be behind the treachery. Frank hadn't had a reason to be suspicious. But now he found himself with doubts creeping into his thinking. He muttered, "Is that asshole making sense about Greene…or am I being played?"

He worried the idea further. That damn lady cop. Maybe she's got him in a squeeze…ha-ha…more ways than one. She wants arrests…lots of unsolved killings. Lookin' at me or Rinaldi or both. She's got to be under some pressure. Goddamn Bob, he's such a pussy. She'll have him handing me over on a silver platter. And fuckin' Rinaldi, he'll be comin' after me soon.

The back door squeaked open and the bartender stuck his head into the room. "Excuse me, Frank. Get you something? I'm setting up for some personal pizzas. Think you might want one?"

"Thanks, Lou. Let me have one and a cold beer."

"You got it. Get right on it."

Frank sighed and shifted in his seat. He'd have to have proof certain of Greene's betrayal before he accused him or leaned hard on him, or he would reap the wrath of his outfit, as most were loyal to Greene. Also, now that the two hit men had been arrested, would they now turn state's evidence against Greene? Would then Greene be looking for a way out? Would he point the finger at Rinaldi as the original instigator of the Carmine murder, rather than to himself? Or would he stay loyal to Rinaldi and point to Frank as a way out? He knew a lawyer could make a case for either one.

If there was proof positive of Greene's duplicity, how was he to handle the problem? He would have to kill Greene, wouldn't he? Or should he help Bob and the cops in their arrest and subsequent indictment of Greene. No, that would take too long and the outcome uncertain. Either way would be risky and he would have to somehow mitigate this risk if he was to prevent blowback from the outfit. He wondered if he was being played for a fool. That softheaded Bob…is that cop squeezing him?

The next day Frank heard a jail yard attempt to assassinate the two hit men had failed. Did this add credibility to Bob's argument? He heard the purported hit men, Joseph Ferrara and Michael Salvini, convinced by the attempt to kill them and by the DA's immediate proposal for a reduced sentence, had changed their plea to guilty of Carmine's murder. The DA's proposal would take the death penalty off the table. Frank expected this event would certainly embroil Greene directly and Rinaldi indirectly in the Carmine/Laura murder. But he knew there was a good chance the hit men would claim they had been in Frank's employ; this to take away any suspicion from Rinaldi. However, a day later, Frank read that the grand jury had heard the DA's evidence against the two suspected hit men, including testimony again by Bob and Gina, and that Ferrara and Salvini were indicted for second-degree murder of Carmine as well as Laura. Bail had been denied. Frank breathed easier.

- - - -

Christy called Bob the day following the indictment of Ferrara and Salvini.

"Bob, just wanted to tell you the two dudes were indicted on second degree murder for both Carmine and Laura."

"I heard on the TV. I was sure glad to hear that."

"I wasn't at all sure it would happen. The evidence was rather sketchy. One other thing just happened."

"What?"

"Greene was found shot dead in his car. Phoenix PD got the call."

"Wow. What's going on?"

"You have anything you can add to that? After all, you and Frank are buds, right?"

Bob hesitated; her voice had a definite edge to it. "I haven't seen or talked to Frank in a while. I don't know anything about what happened to Greene."

"You and Frank talked about it…about your theory of things."

"Sure, but it was just a theory. Frank was pissed and stormed out after we talked about it."

"Bob, you known this won't go away. The DA will surely get involved."

"Yeah…imagine so."

"You'll likely be asked to testify about what you know."

"I really can't add anything substantial. I don't have hard facts."

"If you know anything at all about the hit on Greene, you'll need to come forward."

"I don't have direct knowledge about that. Suspicions, yes. Frank never talked to me after we had the meeting."

"Bob, I'm disappointed but not surprised. Take care of yourself."

Christy hung up without further comment.

Bob was on his second cup of coffee the following morning when the phone rang.

"Hi Christy. What's happening?"

"I just want you to know how important I think it would be for you to give evidence of Frank's involvement in Greene's murder. I don't say this without understanding your relationship with him, but I'm trying to see justice done here."

Bob paused to ponder his response. "I don't have direct information about the murder of Greene and I'm not going to pursue this with Frank. He'd never tolerate it. I'm sure he'd see it as a threat and it wouldn't be healthy for me."

"I had hoped you might have changed your mind. I understand what you're saying, but I think you may have made a pact with the devil."

"All I ever wanted was to see justice for Laura's murder. I've achieved it and I am no longer in Frank's domain. He and I haven't spoken since our meeting."

"Well, I can't argue with you. Please stay safe."

"Thanks, Christy." The line went dead.

When he called her later, hoping to reason with her, he received only phone mail.

CHAPTER 27
POST INDICTMENTS

During the following week Bob and Greg talked about reorganizing the company to address investigating cases of fraud separately from that of other criminal activity. The workload had increased substantially in the past month and their response had slowed noticeably. Bob and Greg felt the pressure from clients for more rapid results.

"It's getting hard to keep up with all the requests we're getting," said Bob.

Greg chuckled. "Yeah, there's only one of me."

"Indeed and I've been laid up a lot."

"Have you thought anymore about hiring a secretary?" asked Greg. "A lot of what we do is paper work and filing and reports."

Bob nodded a few times. "Going over the books last night, I can't justify hiring a regular secretary."

"How about a high school kid? There must be some that can read and write."

Bob chuckled. "I had the same thought." He took a long sip from his coffee and then cleared his throat. "I'll tell you what I'm thinking. I'd like to give you a permanent position with responsibility for all the state and insurance fraudster investigations."

Greg grinned. "Seriously?"

"Well, I do have a condition attached to that."

"Huh?"

"I'd like you to go ahead and pursue Law Enforcement at the Jr. College. I'd be willing to pay half the college tuition. Think you could handle that and work here also?"

"You bet," exclaimed Greg. "I would really appreciate that opportunity. Thanks."

"I'm thinking this arrangement could let me focus on investigative work for domestic criminal and civil suits. This way as each of our groups grow we can add help where needed. What do you think?"

Greg was smiling. "I like it. I'll definitely go after the Law Enforcement courses, and then maybe on to the University."

"That's what I wanted to hear. Let's shake on it."

The two men got up and shook on the plans.

As Bob sat back at his desk he looked at Greg. "You might want to reorganize the outer office to provide you some measure of privacy for clients as they arrive. Also, look at what office equipment is out there and what you will need in the near term. We can order what you need from the Internet."

"Great. I'll give it some thought. I'm headed out right now; got a couple fraudsters to chase down."

"Okay. I'll catch up with you later."

Greg picked up a satchel and left the office. Bob sat at his desk smiling and typed out an email to Christy outlining the plans that he and Greg had shook hands on.

CHAPTER 28

POST TRIAL

Bob sat at his desk glancing through the morning newspaper. The murder of Greene went unsolved, as no witness had been found. Bob had declined to make public his previous conversations with Frank. Christy had discontinued her intimate relationship with Bob and had not returned his recent calls. He knew she now had another unsolved case on her record, but he took solace in some justice for Laura.

He read where the DA had requested an expedited trial of the two suspects, as fear for their lives in the jail population was high. Both the DA and Public Defender for the suspects agreed to terms for an early trial. The two men had decided to plead no contest. The trials held before a judge resulted in a quick conviction of the two men for second-degree murder of Carmine as well as Laura, and were sentenced to forty years to life in state prison. Bob and Gina gave witness testimony of their conversation with Laura. No direct evidence had been presented at the trial by the defense linking Rinaldi or Palumbo to the two hit men or to the crimes. With the two hit men likely to spend their lives in prison, Bob felt some degree of justice for Laura.

An article on page three of the paper stated from undisclosed sources that Frank would continue as head of the Palumbo as no challenge was expected at this time from either law enforcement of from within the outfit.

When the phone rang he was glad to see the call was from Christy.

"Hi Christy, happy to hear from you."

"I guess you're feeling a little bit vindicated, huh?"

"The trial went as well as one could hope for. I feel there was some justice for Laura."

"Okay. Just to let you know, the detective division will be working with the DA's office to put together actionable evidence regarding the various unsolved murders that have been linked to the Palumbo outfit."

"There were some that seem suspicious regarding Palumbo people. But I don't have any real evidence about any of these."

"Would you tell me if you came across some information, evidence I could use?"

"I would. Yes. I sure wouldn't hold it back."

"Even if it's regarding Frank?"

"Christy, I've said it before; I don't owe Frank anything."

"Okay. I really hope you don't become an adversary in the effort to nail Palumbo for his crimes."

"You don't have to worry about that. I haven't talked to Frank since the two goons were indicted."

"Okay. I really care about you, Bob." She disconnected.

A little while later Greg came into the office to pick up his satchel and camera. He sat for a few minutes to catch up with Bob. "Anything new in the paper about the Palumbo's?"

"I'm reading this gossip column. The guy says Frank brought two strong talents in from Chicago to expanded business and revenues."

"Yeah, I can imagine what that means," said Greg.

"Says here that Frank told this reporter that he wants to stay clear of the drug business."

"How's he going to do that? All his guys are in it up to their ass."

"Reporter says here in the paper that drug activity won't be sanctioned by Palumbo and no defense will be offered if one of his guys is arrested."

"Yeah well, we'll see how long that lasts. Carmine couldn't stop it."

"Hey, listen to this. Frank says he'll maintain clean financials to avoid income tax issues with the Feds. He hired an accountant to help keep his books."

Greg giggled. "I can just imagine what kind of books he keeps."

"This guy says that Frank bought a controlling interest in a GM auto dealership over in west Phoenix. He picked up an auto parts store also."

"Interesting. The rackets must be doing well."

Bob smiled. "I imagine the cops and FBI will be looking into all of it."

CHAPTER 29
FIRE INSURANCE CLAIM

It was after lunch and Greg was getting ready to try his luck at checking on his list of fraudsters. Bob was again reading the newspaper while he drank his fourth cup of coffee.

"So what do you hear from Christy?" asked Greg. "Does she still talk to you?"

Bob looked up from the newspaper. "I haven't heard from her this week. She seems to think I should be helping her get the bad guys." He shook his head. "I didn't know that was my job, besides what do I know for sure? Damn little."

"Yeah, we can't make stuff up. It happens when it happens."

"She's working with the DA and PD looking at all the past misdeeds linked to Palumbo. Her immediate focus is the bombing of Jack Harvey over by my apartment."

"Odd we haven't heard a peep out of the FBI. After all, it is a federal case isn't it?"

"Well yeah. This Harvey guy was making it with an FBI agent," said Bob.

"It sure sounds like a Palumbo hit, doesn't it?"

Bob put down his coffee cup and nodded. "This affair was going on for a long time, so why now? Why take him out now?"

"What are you thinking?"

"Was it made to look like a Palumbo hit?"

"You mean to throw heat on Palumbo by Rinaldi."

Bob nodded. "I've been wondering about it."

"Makes some sense. Rinaldi wasn't too thrilled when Palumbo moved into Arizona."

"That's right. Could explain some of the bad shit happening around here."

"Okay. I'm headed out."

"Be careful."

Greg waved as he went to the office door.

When Greg arrived at the office the next morning, Bob looked up. "Good morning. By the way, do you have Alfred Dominic on your watch list? I've got an inquiry here from some insurance company."

Greg started to look through papers in his satchel. "Yeah, I do…in here somewhere. Oh yeah, I got him. He's 43 years old, a Palumbo associate, and is suspected of fire insurance fraud."

"Yep, that's him. Apparently, a two-unit apartment owned by Dominic burned down and is insured for $850K. It's in south Scottsdale."

"Okay. What do we know about it?" said Greg.

"Well, the fire inspector said only that the fire was of unknown origin."

Greg shook his head. "Is he waiting for someone to pay him off?"

Bob chuckled. "You have a suspicious mind."

"I wonder where I got that from."

"By the way, this Dominic guy requested immediate payment. Insurance company is asking us for a background investigation on this guy. They want us to look at stuff that might not be available to the PD and would be useful to sue Dominic. So you need to put this guy on top of your list."

"Okay. No problem. I'll see what I can dig up on him. A while back I had him hooked up with one of the Rinaldi guys. This Rinaldi dude had purchased volatile chemicals and it was suspected Dominic burned down a store, maybe accidentally. It seemed suspicious as some of the chemicals were what's used in drug processing."

"Okay, do your thing. I'll send an e-mail to Christy alerting her on what you're doing."

A few minutes later Bob's phone rang.

"Hi Christy, it's nice to hear from you."

"Uh-huh. Reason I called is about this Dominic guy. You sent Greg out to investigate him?"

"Yes, Dominic is on top of his list."

"We have him in our sights as well. You're working with Southwest Fire and Casualty?"

"Yes, they asked us to check him out as they want to get ready to sue him."

"Okay. Just want to be sure you let Greg know we know him as a dangerous and violent man. He should be very careful."

"Thanks. I'll be sure to tell him. I'll call him."

"Good. I've gotta go. Take care." The call was dropped.

Bob felt some sadness as he put the phone down.

CHAPTER 30
GREG HELD CAPTIVE

When Greg stepped out of the office building to the parking lot he was immediately accosted by two men he didn't know. He dropped his satchel and tried to ward off several blows before a gag was tied over his mouth and he was shoved to a nearby car. In the back seat he was jammed between the two thugs heavy with body odor. The car sped north on side streets and finally turned north on Scottsdale Road headed toward the McDowell Mountains. His mumbled protests went unanswered as the car sped north. Greg kept asking to where they were taking him. They finally admitted that he was being taken to some place north of the McDowell Mountains to be held until however long the grand jury is in session. Upon further questioning, he was told Alfred Dominic had ordered his capture. It was then that the driver ordered the two thugs next to Greg to shut their mouths.

Greg began to fear for his life. He realized he was being held to prevent his testifying against Dominic. He knew the grand jury might be in session for weeks more and these thugs might well want to be rid of him. He was frightened at that prospect and decided he'd have to make an escape attempt as he was convinced no one would know where he was being held. In a half hour they ran out of paved road and were now on a dusty and bumpy two track into the desert northwest of the mountains. Another twenty minutes and the car stopped near a weathered and dilapidated shack. The window and door were mere openings in the bleached plank walls.

Treachery | 153

"Where the hell are we?" asked Greg.

"Here's your new home, asshole. Get out and make yourself comfy inside."

The driver got out of the car and barked an order. "Search him first. Bring me his ID and phone."

One ruffian held Greg while the other searched him. His wallet and phone were given to the driver, clearly the boss of the operation. The man looked through the phone data, and unimpressed tossed the phone on the ground. Also, after a quick look, the wallet was tossed after the phone.

Greg saw a wooden platform covering what he suspected was an old mine shaft. Several large rocks had been placed on top of the structure presumably to discourage the curious. One thug shoved Greg toward the shack and then both went inside. Seconds later the other ruffian entered with a handful of plastic strip-ties and they proceed to bind Greg's ankles. They left his arms unencumbered with a warning to not try to escape because a bullet would find him before he got very far. Greg despaired at how he could escape.

"I have to pee," said Greg.

"Hobble your way to the door and let 'er go."

The other thug found it funny and almost choked laughing.

Greg, humiliated, took tiny steps and without falling got to the door. He saw the driver wave his arms and yell. "Get back inside." Greg cursed and proceeded to shoot a stream in the man's direction before turning around and hobbling back to the far wall.

"I'm thirsty. I need something to eat."

"Too bad. Just shut the hell up. Maybe Carlo will bring something."

Shit, another guy coming? This ain't good. He slid his back down the wall to sit on the floor. A feeling of despair came over him.

- - - - -

When Bob stepped outside that afternoon to go to his car, he saw Greg's satchel lying on the ground. He picked it up and looked inside to be sure it belonged to Greg. Then panic gripped him. He pulled his phone from his pocket and called Christy.

"Bob, what's up?"

"Something's happened to Greg. He left the building around noon, but I just found his satchel lying in the parking lot. His car is still here. Jesus, I don't know where to look for him. I'm scared…what could have happened?"

"Okay. Slow down. Take some deep breaths. You sent him out to investigate this Alfred Dominic guy?"

"Yes. It was top of his list."

"I'm going to put together some officers that'll help with a search. You stay where you are. I'll be over in twenty minutes."

"Okay. I don't know where to look."

"Wait for me." Christy disconnected.

Bob kept walking around the parking lot while trying to figure where Greg could be and who had taken him. His heart raced and he perspired. The thought of Greg in mortal danger frightened him. Christy arrived after twenty minutes.

"Bob, stop. Here, lean against my car. Jesus, you look terrible."

"I gotta find him."

"We will. I have several officers asking around on some good sources. Something will turn up. Now tell me what you and Greg were talking about just before he left."

Bob ran his hand over his face and shook his head. "I don't remember, just the different cases he was working on."

"You were talking about this Alfred Dominic guy, weren't you?"

Bob rubbed his face again. "I…uh."

"Think, Bob! Weren't you guys talking about Greg checking on Dominic?"

"Bob nodded. "Yes…Yes we were. He was going to check on him today."

"Okay." Christy reached into her cruiser and pulled up the microphone. There was a short conversation that sent a patrol to find Dominic and search his immediate area. "Now listen to me, Bob."

Bob looked at her and blinked several times.

"I'm going back to the office. I will be communicating with my officers out on the street. We will keep looking for Greg. I suggest going back inside and wait in your office until I call you with an update. Can you do that?"

Bob nodded and took Greg's satchel from the hood of the cruiser and went to the building entrance. As he opened the door, he heard Christy's cruiser drive off rapidly. He went up the stairs to his office and sat at his desk. Minutes ticked by before he remembered his encounter some days ago.

It was the threat in Rinaldi's limo that he would end up in the bottom of a mineshaft for pursuing his investigations. He sat straight up in his seat. A chill ran through his body. He woke up his idling computer and first searched the National Forest web site for mining claim sites in the Scottsdale/Phoenix area. Dissatisfied with that search he went to search mining claim records in Arizona. After ten minutes he focused on old mining claims north of Scottsdale in the McDowell Mountain area and copied a map of the location of old mine claims. He mused that this area offered the highest probability for the Rinaldi gangsters to dispose of bodies. Again he thought of the threat made to him in the back of the limo.

He made a quick decision and changed his business clothes to jeans and sneakers and a dark t-shirt. He wouldn't say anything to Christy…not yet. She would talk him out of it…but not yet; he had to be sure.

He picked up the phone and called Ricky, a young man he had helped stay out of jail.

"Hey Ricky, its Bob Wagner."

"Yeah Bob, what's happening."

"I could use your help. You still have that cool drone we flew last year?"

"Sure. Got a new one too."

"Could you loan me the one I used last year. I kinda know how to operate it."

"Ah…Yeah. You're not going to break it, are you?"

"No problem. I'll give you a twenty for your troubles."

"Okay. Come get it. You'll have it back in a day or so?"

"Yep. I will. I'll take care of it."

"Okay. You know where I live."

"Be there in thirty minutes." Bob hung up.

The phone rang as soon as he had hung up.

"Bob Wagner."

"Bob, this is Frank. Got some news you want to hear."

"Can it wait? My man Greg has gone missing. I have to go look for him."

Frank's response sounded to Bob as a growl. "Wagner! Get your head on straight! You listening to me?"

"Okay, Frank. Sorry. I'm a little rattled."

"Sit your ass down and listen to what I gotta say." He sounded more normal.

"Okay Frank. I'm at my desk."

"I got people. I hear things. Now listen. Your man was taken by some of Rinaldi's goons up to the McDowell Mountains area. Where exactly, I don't know. All my guy could get was your guy was being held at the old Hermit Mine, wherever the hell that is. Its someplace those goons take people they want to disappear. There's some kind of shack there and a deep mineshaft. I don't know anything else. Did you hear what I'm sayin' to you?"

"Jesus, yes…thanks very much, Frank. I'm gonna go look for him up that way."

"Well, Dick Tracy, you going to find that place…you better bring some back up. Those goons will be armed and waiting for trouble. This guy, he knows those assholes. Maybe its time for your lady cop to earn her salary."

"Yeah. Thanks Frank." He disconnected.

Bob spent a few minutes looking at the McDowell Mountains area map he had printed. Then from his desk he grabbed his gun and a spare ammunition clip and headed for his car. Eight minutes later he pulled up in front of Ricky's house. He was waiting for him in front of the open garage.

Ricky smiled, "Got it all ready for ya."

Bob opened his wallet and pulled out a twenty-dollar bill and handed it to Ricky. "This puppy works like it did last year?"

Rick brought the drone from the garage and they set it on the passenger side front seat.

"Hey, it's in perfect shape. It has a new set of batteries. All you do is crank up the computer and off it goes."

"I forget. What's the range?"

"It'll go for 1000 meters. Don't try to go farther or you'll lose it. That'll cost you a hell of a lot more than a twenty."

They both laughed about that, but Bob was anxious to get going. He had operated the drone before and knew its parameters.

They waved to each other as Bob got into his SUV and drove off.

Bob drove to the McDowell Mountains leaving paved roads miles behind. When he arrived within a mile of where he thought the Hermit Mine was located, he stopped by a clump of brush at the base of a group of hills. On the hood of the vehicle he readied the drone and computer to search in a loop to the west and south and then to return. The afternoon was rapidly waning; there wasn't any time to waste. He had to find Greg before dark.

It was at dusk when Bob found the mine mentioned by Frank. On the computer screen he saw there was a vehicle nearby. But he didn't see anyone. The old shack looked to have been well visited as the ground was disturbed with tire tracks. The old shaft had a dilapidated wooden cover. The shack itself looked like it could collapse in a good wind. He saw the visibility from the shack was mostly to the south and southwest. An eastern approach would be safest. To the north were some rugged hills that he decided to avoid.

The drone returned and Bob prepared to investigate the shack immediately. He decided to explore around the shack without telling Christy just yet. He wanted to be certain that Greg was still being held there.

CHAPTER 31
GREG RESCUED

Bob crept up to the shack at dusk and could hear voices of two men. Greg was heard a few times. Bob crept close to the single window with drawn pistol. The window at one time had contained glass panes but now was just a big opening.

He heard an exclamation from one of the thugs about hearing noise outside. Bob moved quickly to escape to the north into brush but they had seen him. Two gunshots sounded. Bob found shelter in the dark shadows of a deep ravine choked with brush. The two thugs apparently were afraid to approach in the increasing darkness. A few minutes later another shot rang out and splattered in the rocks very close to Bob.

Having seen the flash, Bob returned a shot in that direction. Another shot landed very close to Bob. Bob pulled his phone from his pocket, and covering the illuminated screen with his hand, he dialed 911. The call was answered by a dispatch center and he asked for Scottsdale PD. On being connected, he asked for Christy.

"Bob! Where are you?"

"I'm at a place known as the Hermit Mine. It's on the west side of the McDowell Mountains. I'm getting shot at. They're holding Greg here. I need some help."

"Jesus, Bob. How did you find out about Greg? He's there? You sure?"

Two shots rang out and splattered in the nearby rocks.

"Who's shooting? Bob, what's going on?"

"Christy, I need help. Can you get me some help?"

"Yes. I have two patrols and the sheriff headed toward you now. Can you stay on the phone?"

Bob turned off the phone and stuffed it back in his pocket.

Bob snuck back to the shack approaching it down the gully to the west. He hoped the shack would be empty of goons so he could rescue Greg. When he got there he saw Greg in the near dark of the shack, tied and lying on the floor against the far wall.

"Greg…Greg are you hurt?"

"Bob? How'd you find me? I'm sure glad to see you. Those bastards will be back any minute."

As Bob tried to undo the ties on his ankles, they heard the thugs outside yelling for him to come out. That was followed by a round of shots coming through the window and the door opening.

"Son of a bitch!" yelled Greg. "They're gonna rush us!"

"Lay down on the floor. It ain't over yet."

Lying on the floor to one side of the doorway, Bob took aim at where he saw movement in the brush and fired several shots. A scream and vulgar yelling ensued. A volley of shots ripped through the walls into the shack and Bob was hit in the right shoulder. He dropped his pistol but then recovered it. He was in sharp pain but was still able to handle the pistol.

"Bob! You're hit!"

"Stay down. Don't give them a target. I think there are more of those bastards out there."

Greg was on the floor struggling frantically with his ankle bindings. Bob saw the arrival of car headlights and soon realized more thugs had arrived. Vulgar yells preceded additional shots that slammed into the shack.

It was then they heard loudspeaker voices demanding the gunmen put down their weapons and raise their hands. There were several volleys of shots and then all was quiet. In what seemed to Bob as an eternity, a minute later several deputies with flashlights entered the shack to discover Bob leaning against the wall at the doorway with a bloody shoulder wound and Greg lying on the floor against the back wall still trying to undo the ties around his ankles.

Suddenly Bob saw Christy in the doorway.

Christy arrived and was shocked at the scene. She went to Bob to comfort him, all angst seemingly forgotten. "What happened?"

She looked over at Greg. "Greg, are you hurt?"

He shook his head. "No…Is Bob okay?"

"We'll take him to the trauma center in Fountain Hills. You sure you're okay?"

"Oh Bob, how did you find Greg?"

"It was Frank."

Her eyes widened. "What? Frank? What the hell?"

"He called… gave me a tip."

"A tip? How'd he know? Was he involved? Damn it Bob."

"No, no. He heard about this from some guy he knows. Called me."

She shook her head and watched as the EMTs prepared Bob for transport to the trauma center.

Greg volunteered he was well enough to drive Bob's SUV back home. Christy agreed.

Frank called Bob that evening at the hospital.

"Hey, it's Frank. Can you talk?"

"Yep. Hey, thanks for the tip. It sure worked out."

"Yeah, well, I've got ears all over the place and people owe me. I figured I better tell you before those morons took out your main man."

"Greg is okay. I got clipped in the shoulder."

"No shit? You got hit? Sorry to hear that."

"Yeah. It sure hurts."

"By the way, did the cops ever show up?"

"I called before I engaged them. Figured I needed all the help I could get."

"Your lady cop show up?"

"She did. When I told her that you gave me a tip, she got all pissed."

"Yeah, well, okay."

"They'll send me home tomorrow with a cast on my shoulder."

"At least you're in one piece. See ya around."

"Yeah, thanks."

Greg brought Bob home from the trauma center before noon the next day. They exchanged stories of the previous night's episode. A news team waited outside Bob's apartment asking to be brought up to date. When asked who would do such a vile thing Bob suggested the bad guys were likely working for Romano and was part of the Rinaldi outfit. After a few minutes Bob excused himself and went inside.

Christy visited at noon. She wanted to hear all about the previous days events from Greg and Bob.

"How did you find the mine in the evening? It was almost dark by then."

"Frank told me he thought Greg was being held at the Hermit Mine. Apparently it's some place where the mob people take undesirables to make them disappear."

"Yeah, you told me. How did you find it out there in the near dark?"

"I borrowed a drone with a camera from a friend. He and I had played with it last year and I knew what it could do."

Christy shook her head.

"What? I was able to find the place quickly once I launched the drone."

"It just sounds too fantastical. A drone?"

"The PD surely has some, don't they?"

She shook her head. "I don't think so." She took notes as they talked, for a report, she said.

Greg spoke up. "I overheard two of the thugs talking about holding me during the grand jury session, however long that lasted, so I couldn't testify and do damage to Rinaldi."

"Christy, you think the PD has enough to bring charges against Rinaldi himself?" asked Bob.

Christy grimaced. "Maybe. The DA will have to review the evidence and our guys are still working on that."

"I don't mind saying, I became rather worried about my life," said Greg. "Particularly if the process went on much longer. I didn't get a good feeling from how those bastards were talking. I kept thinking about that mine shaft outside the cabin and wondering how many poor slobs were at the bottom."

"That's a good thought," said Christy. "I'll ask for a crew to check on what's down there.

"I think we owe Frank a lot for the tip. It sure saved the day," said Bob looking at Greg.

"I am very uncomfortable with this Frank thing," said Christy. "How the hell he'd know about the Hermit Mine... and that Greg was there? Are you telling me everything?"

Bob shrugged. "I didn't ask him that. I was just grateful for the tip."

"And what, you jumped on your horse Silver and galloped out there like the Lone Ranger? You didn't call the PD for support?" Christy shook her head. "You're one strange guy."

"I did what I had to do. I wasn't going to call the PD without first knowing if Greg was out there…if Frank's tip was good."

Christy smiled. "I understand you, but I don't agree with you."

CHAPTER 32
RINALDI FIGHTS BACK

The following morning Bob picked up the phone and heard Frank's gruff voice.

"This is Frank. You okay?"

"Uncomfortable, but I'm at the office. Like I told you, I got winged."

"Yeah. Listen, you know I've got ears all over."

"That's what you said."

"This guy tells me Rinaldi is enraged at what happened at the mine. He's been talking about making an effort to get you out of the way before the grand jury gets to hear from you."

"Oh hell, the grand jury may not even call on me. Besides, I'm not anxious to be a hero."

"Like I said, he's rippin' mad and you've humiliated him out there at the mine. If I were you I would assume he's gonna do what he's boasting about to his guys."

"Okay, Frank. I appreciate the warning. I'm keeping my man Greg close to home. I don't want anything else to happen to him."

"Yeah, whatever. What I heard is that he mentioned you specifically. So be advised."

"Thanks, Frank."

"Yeah. Watch your ass."

Bob hung up and sat back in his chair. At the moment he was more angry than scared. He had a job to do and he couldn't let himself be scared of Rinaldi. Well, he'd keep Greg in the office, no point in putting him in danger again.

He picked up the phone and pushed the number for Christy.

"Hey Bob, what's happening?"

"I received another warning from Frank."

"Frank, huh? What is it this time?"

"He told me he heard from a spy he uses that Rinaldi is enraged at what happened at the mine. Apparently he's been heard talking about getting me out of the way, whatever that means, before the grand jury hears from me."

"You think Frank's on the level?"

"He's been giving me good stuff so far."

"What did he suggest you do?"

"His parting words were 'watch your ass.'"

"Doesn't sound very helpful."

"Well, in Frank speak, it probably means to expect trouble from behind…an ambush maybe."

"The PD can't help you without a specific threat. What you need is a bodyguard."

"Financially, that's out of the question. I'm keeping Greg in the office now while I do the investigative tasks. I can't bear to have him get hurt again."

"I understand. He's been through enough. You could hire an off duty police officers for certain days or times. Maybe you could afford that?"

"I may do that. I'll think about it. Just thought I'd run this by you."

"Bob, you're making me crazy with all the drama these days. I don't want to see you in the morgue. It's what I keep worrying about."

"You're right. Enough with the drama."

"Be careful. Watch your back."

When they hung up Bob sat back in his chair. He was scared but decided that he couldn't live with this threat hanging over him and Greg. A proactive stance is what he intended to do in order to get proof positive of Alfred Dominic's propensity for fire insurance fraud.

Next he called Greg.

"Hey Bob, what's happening?"

"I received a call from Frank, basically warning me to watch my back as he heard Rinaldi was ripping mad about what happened out there at the mine. I just talked to Christy but nothing much came of that. I want you to stay in the office for a while until things calm down. I will go out and do the field-work to keep the fraudsters in check."

"But why? You think they're still coming after me?"

"I don't know. I just can't stand to think of you in anymore danger."

"Hell, you're in danger too. There's probably a bounty on your head."

"Maybe. I want you in the office. Understand?"

"Yeah, I got it. It doesn't feel right to me, though."

"Humor me, for a while anyhow."

"Okay. I'll be in later."

Before Greg came into the office, Bob prepared to visit a possible fire insurance fraud site. Southwest Fire and Casualty stated they were waiting for the fire inspectors report but in the meantime they asked for Confidential Investigations to inspect the property and send in a report.

Bob decided to go armed when he was out of the building and to use the 911 feature on his phone if the situation became dangerous. He discussed his plan with Christy before he left. She was dismayed at events and hoped the PD could be there to help him if needed. She promised to increase patrols at his office and apartment.

The burned out hulk of the two-family rental on Swanson Street in east Phoenix and owned by Alfred Dominic was surrounded by yellow Keep Out tape. Bob didn't see anyone on the property and decided to get a close-up view of the remains. He stooped under the tape and readied his phone camera as he walked toward the foul smelling mess. Bob saw it was a nice neighborhood and thought the insurance claim of $850K was not an excessive valuation. Although the fire inspector had reported the fire was of unknown origin, Bob knew Dominic's history of fire insurance fraud.

He walked methodically around the building inspecting the burned remains. He observed the furnace and water heater were both gas-fired units and he looked carefully at the remains. The metal housings of both units were distorted from severe heat. The remaining floor timbers above were charred black. Other timbers, although burned, had not received nearly as much heat. Bob took photos with his phone of the various burn features and close-in features of the furnace and water heater. On completing a circuit around the remains, he went back to the furnace and water heater and looked closely at the pipes that fed the natural gas to the units. Rough tool marks were still visible on the coupling hardware at the connection of the two units to the gas feed line coming into the building. The copper pipe from the hot water heater had been twisted to nearly shut off the flow of gas. This was certainly not a normal thing to expect and Bob suspected the pipe may have been fractured.

Bob did not go into the basement as that would definitely be against all regulations, but he took more photos of the damaged piping at the furnace and water heater. He thought that the thin walled copper pipe could have easily been cracked in the severe twisting by someone with use of a wrench. He was tempted to go into the basement, but caution won out.

Sitting back in his car, Bob recorded his observations into a solid-state voice recorder. Just as he was ready to depart, a Phoenix police patrol stopped behind him with light bar turned on. Bob turned off the engine, lowered the window and waited for the officer to approach.

The officer stood there for several seconds and looked at Bob without saying anything. Then he asked, "Sir, why are you stopped here?"

"I'm an investigator at Confidential Investigations for Southwest Fire and Casualty." Bob removed his identification and driver license and held it at the window. "I needed to see what was left of the building and report it to the company."

The officer took the cards handed to him and withdrew back to his patrol car. Bob sat quietly occasionally glancing at the rearview mirror. It seemed to be an excessively long time before the officer returned and handed Bob his cards.

"Mr. Wagner, did you find what you were looking for?"

Bob was prepared for the misleading question. "I needed to see what was left of the building and report it to Southwest Fire and Casualty."

"You are not to cross the yellow tape barrier, sir."

"Okay. I understand."

"Do you?"

Bob nodded. "I do."

"Have a good day. Drive Safe."

As the officer went back to his car, Bob toyed with the radio setting to let a minute go by. The officer had not left so Bob started his car and drove off. He headed back toward Scottsdale on Shea Boulevard and nervously checked his rearview mirror. It was late morning and traffic was moderate. As he approached Scottsdale Road he realized he had picked up a tail. He made a right turn to the next street and there turned left to continue to Scottsdale Road. The tail was still behind him. A chill went up his body, glad he had his gun under his sport coat and the officer hadn't sensed it. Before reaching Scottsdale Road another car merged in front of him and forced him to brake as the other car slowed quickly. He realized he was now hemmed in between to cars and they were stopped. Light traffic passed by and the two other cars remained stopped. What the hell is going on? Are the assholes trying to get me to get out of my car? Bob reached for his phone and pressed Christy's number. It rang twice.

"Hello, Bob?"

"Yes. I think I'm in a bit of a bind. I have a car blocking me in front and another blocking me in back. So far no one has made a move, but I can't move my car. Something is going to happen."

"Damn it Bob, where the heck are you?"

"I'm east bound on Wilbur just west of Scottsdale Road. Can you have a patrol come by?"

"Don't leave your car. Lock your doors. I'll have a patrol check on you. It'll be a few minutes."

"Okay. Thanks."

Now disconnected, he put the phone on the seat, disturbed by Christy's hard voice. He again felt the gun at his chest, hoping he wouldn't have to use it. Several minutes ticked by and there wasn't any movement from either car and no police evident. A black Mercedes suddenly stopped on the driver's side of Bob's car. Bob was shocked when a large man left the Mercedes and came to Bob's door, a pistol in his hand. Suddenly he saw a man leave the car blocking him in front as well as another from the car at the rear; both carried pistols at their sides. Bob pulled his gun from the holster and took off the safety. A few cars whizzed by like an ordinary day, but Bob was very afraid. He didn't see any police.

A gun butt smashed into the passenger side window sending glass into the cabin. Immediately, the driver side window was smashed. Pieces of glass showered over Bob. The passenger door was unlocked and pulled open and two sweaty faces screamed at him to get out of the car. Bob didn't move and suddenly from behind claws grabbed at Bob's throat and squeezed. With a rush of panic and adrenaline, Bob turned his pistol against the driver's door and pulled the trigger. The fingers relaxed just as a shot tore into him from the open passenger door. He turned and fired, squeezing off three shots as pain overwhelmed him. He could hear a commotion of sirens and loudspeakers, but he was losing consciousness. He struggled to stay alert, but then gave up.

CHAPTER 33
SETTLEMENT

All he could remember was the pain as people moved him out of the car and into an ambulance. He had no recollection of anything else. He awoke in a bright hospital room, realized where he was and closed his eyes again. He wondered what day it was. Images danced in his mind as he tried to understand what had happened. He recognized nurses around him and wondered what they said. He drifted in and out of sleep and heard people come to his bed and then leave again.

He was jarred awake as his bed was being moved; then into an elevator, and then up to another floor. The air felt cold. Finally, he was in another room. Nurses did things with his bed and the medical equipment on a pole next to him. The room got darker. What was happening? He moved his toes and his fingers and found relief in knowing his limbs were still functioning. Then he slid into sleep again.

The room was brighter now. He opened his eye slightly. It was quiet. Was this a different day? He moved his hands down his body and felt a tube at his side. What the hell was that, he wondered? He again checked to make sure his fingers and toes still functioned. Relieved, he closed his eyes.

The room had become a little darker when he awoke to talking near his bed. He forced his eyes open and saw Christy and Greg and two nurses. The nurses left. Greg went up to Bob's bed. "Hey, he's awake."

Christy bent over and looked at Bob, placing her hand on his face. She said something that he couldn't understand. She bent over again and kissed his forehead. He slowly pulled an arm from under the blanket and gripped Christy's hand. He heard questions and talk but he couldn't get his mind together. He tried to smile. The nurses came back, and then everyone was gone again. He closed his eyes.

Bob opened his eyes the next morning to see Christy and Greg at his bedside. He stared at them and then focused on Christy.

"Glad you guys here."

"Oh Bob, you had us very worried." She bent over and kissed his cheek.

Greg moved closer. "Wow, I'm sure glad you pulled through. Good that you're awake."

Bob rubbed his face. "How long have I been here? I don't remember much."

"This is day three," said Christy. "Doctor wants you to go to a rehab place."

Greg bent closer. "I told them I could take care of you at your office since you have a bedroom. The doctor wasn't real keen with that."

"You mean they want me to go to another place…a rehab place?"

"I'll be talking to the doctor," said Christy. "I think Greg's idea is good."

Bob looked from Christy to Greg and back again. "Why…what is wrong with me?"

"You don't remember?" asked Christy. "You were shot in your car."

Bob stared at her. "What…what happened?"

"You don't remember anything?"

"Some things…guy broke my window…started choking me."

"You shot him," blurted Greg.

"I shot him…?"

"You did," said Christy. "It was Tony Romano."

Bob stared at her. "Really? I shot him?"

Christy nodded. "He's dead."

Bob fell silent for a few seconds. "Romano? I killed him?"

"Shot him right through the car door," exclaimed Greg.

Christy shook her head. "They couldn't save him. Bled out internally."

"You shot another guy at the passenger door," said Greg. "He's alive. Remember him?"

"I think so. There were two of them."

"Detectives say you fired three shots, one through the driver's door, two shots at the guys at the passenger door. You hit on of those guys. He'll pull through."

"Jesus…"

Christy continued. "You took a bullet from one of the guys at the passenger door that went into your lower chest, broke a rib, took out some lung tissue and ended up in the car door. You were rather lucky, all in all. I think they patched you up. They're still concerned with possible infection. They had a drain placed in your chest. I guess it's out now."

"When can I get out of here?"

"Don't worry about anything," said Greg. "So far, I've got all the customers taken care of."

"I sure owe you. Thanks for all that."

"Greg and I will be talking with the doctor on our way out," said Christy. "We'll press him hard to let you stay with Greg at your office."

Bob nodded a few times.

"Hang in there," said Greg. "We'll be talking to you, maybe tomorrow morning."

Christy bent over and kissed Bob on the cheek. "We'll call."

They left the room and Bob settled in his bed, sleep overtaking him. A nurse came in and greeted him and then made some adjustments to the medication equipment by his bed.

It was late in the afternoon when there was a knock at the door to his room. Bob was awake and lying quietly thinking about all that had happened. He ignored the knock. The door was pushed open slowly and Bob saw Frank's head poke in.

"Hey, is it okay to come in?"

"Frank? Yeah, come in."

Frank walked in and was followed by an older heavyset man of Frank's height.

"Bob, now don't get your balls in a knot, I want you to meet Carlos Rinaldi."

"What the hell…?"

"Just listen to me for a minute… Will you do that?"

"What is this?" Bob was a bit frightened and confused.

"Bob, listen to me. I got to thinking about that theory of yours. All this stuff with Rick Greene and Tony Romano and now this shooting you were involved in, holy crap. Greene is dead and now you took Romano off the board. I got to thinking about all this and got a hold of Carlos and we had a few drinks and we talked about what happened and about what you said."

"So? What are you telling me?"

"What I'm sayin' is Carlos and I agree all this violence and shit that's happened isn't any good for either of us. We think Greene and Romano have been working for some time to get both of our outfits so fucked up to where they could take control of them. All the bombings and assassinations were not part of either of our plans, they were Greene and Romano plans."

Bob shook his head. "You shittin' me?"

"You know, we're business guys. Carlos has his thing and I have mine. We both want to steer clear of the feds and the IRS and grow our business. There's never been any reason for us not to get along and maybe even work together. All this shit that's been going on…it ends now."

"It ends now," Carlos repeated.

"Maria? What happens to her?"

Frank glanced at Carlos. "She's definitely a loose end. She's better off back in Chicago. That place where she lives now will be sold as part of Carmine's estate. She won't be welcome around here."

"This is so damn confusing." Bob shook his head.

The two men went to the door. Frank said, "Bob, we want to wish you well. There's no hard feelin's."

Carlos nodded, "No hard feelin's."

Seconds later both men had left and Bob lay back on the pillow trying to understand what had just happened.

CHAPTER 34

FINALE

It was ten o'clock the next morning when Greg and Christy knocked and entered Bob's room. A nurse was just completing taking a blood sample. When she left the room Christy and Greg crowded around Bob's bed.

Christy bent over and kissed his cheek. Greg stood next to her grinning.

"Good to see you guys."

"Did you sleep well?" asked Christy.

"Well…I had visitors yesterday. That kept me awake for a while after they left."

Christy and Greg stared at Bob. Christy said, "What visitors?"

"There was a knock at the door and before I answered Frank came in and brought a long another guy."

"Frank Palumbo? Who came with him?" said Christy.

Greg stared at him expectantly.

"Frank brought Carlos Rinaldi. I couldn't believe my eyes."

"Wow. Rinaldi?" said Greg.

"Really? Rinaldi here?" Christy was almost speechless. "Wha…What did they want?"

"Apparently, Frank has been rethinking what has happened now that Green and Romano are dead."

"What do you mean?" Christy seemed perplexed.

"All the bombings and killings became suspect in Frank's mind, especially after I talked to him about my theory on things."

"You're kidding."

Bob shook his head. "He decided the state of war between him and Rinaldi didn't need to be. So, he got together with him and worked it out."

Greg was disbelieving. "Worked it out?"

"Frank said he and Carlos agreed the violence and back stabbing that's been happening just isn't good for either of them. I guess they talked about it all and concluded that Greene and Romano have been working all this time to get both outfits so screwed up that they could ultimately get control of them. Turns out, the bombings and murders were not part of either of their plans, they were Greene and Romano plans."

"Holy crap," exclaimed Greg.

"I can't believe this," said Christy. "What, they're buddies now?"

"Not really," said Bob. "They said each had their own business model and they didn't need to compete, maybe even help each other."

Christy shook her head. "Bob, you know how crazy this sounds? What about Maria? What happens to her?"

"I got the impression that was still an issue to be resolved. Frank wants to sell the estate as it's his now. She won't be too welcome around here, as she was in on all the trouble. Better for her if she went back to Chicago."

"Wow. This all happened last evening?" asked Greg.

"Uh-huh. Couldn't go to sleep after that."

"You going to be discharged tomorrow?"

Bob nodded. "They took some more blood today. If it's okay, I leave tomorrow."

Christy came close to Bob's bed. "I suggest we stay together...as a couple. You obviously need a woman in your life to keep you out of trouble."

Greg chuckled and stood back.

Bob smiled and nodded. "I have to agree with you. I want to be with you now more than ever."

"I was thinking for ever."

"Me too."

The End.